The Short Stories of H. Rider Haggard

VOLUME II

Sir Henry Rider Haggard, KBE was born on June 22nd, 1856 at Bradenham in Norfolk, England.

After his education he was pushed towards an Army career but failed the entrance exam. Next Haggard was positioned to work for the British Foreign Office but he seems not to have sat that exam. Using family connections, he was sent to Southern Africa by his father in search of a further opportunity of a career.

Haggard spent six years there before a return to England and marriage. He had begun to write and publish some non-fiction in Africa but it was only after studying Law in the hope it might prove to be the proper career his father wanted for him that Haggard began to write fiction, using his African experiences as the basis.

His first fiction was published in 1885 and the following year King Solomon's Mines was published. It was a phenomenal success. His career was set.

Haggard wrote well and wrote often. He managed to sympathise with the local populations even though they were exploited and manipulated by Europeans intent on amassing fortunes in money, people and resources. His writing career covered the great sprint to Empire of several European powers and both reflects and criticizes these events through his well-loved characters including Allan Quatermain and Ayesha.

In his later years Haggard pursued much in the way social reform as well as standing for Parliament and writing a great many letters to The Times.

Henry Rider Haggard died on May 14th, 1925 at the age of 68. His ashes were buried at Ditchingham Church.

Index of Contents

Chapter VI

Chapter I

Philip Hadden and King Cetywayo

At the date of our introduction to him, Philip Hadden was a transport- rider and trader in "the Zulu." Still on the right side of forty, in appearance he was singularly handsome; tall, dark, upright, with keen eyes, short-pointed beard, curling hair and clear-cut features. His life had been varied, and there were passages in it which he did not narrate even to his most intimate friends. He was of gentle birth, however, and it was said that he had received a public school and university education in England. At any rate he could quote the classics with aptitude on occasion, an accomplishment which, coupled with his refined voice and a bearing not altogether common in the wild places of the world, had earned for him among his rough companions the soubriquet of "The Prince."

However these things may have been, it is certain that he had emigrated to Natal under a cloud, and equally certain that his relatives at home were content to take no further interest in his fortunes. During the fifteen or sixteen years which he had spent in or about the colony, Hadden followed many trades, and did no good at any of them. A clever man, of agreeable and prepossessing manner, he always found it easy to form friendships and to secure a fresh start in life. But, by degrees, the friends were seized with a vague distrust of him; and, after a period of more or less application, he himself would close the opening that he had made by a sudden disappearance from the locality, leaving behind him a doubtful reputation and some bad debts.

Before the beginning of this story of the most remarkable episodes in his life, Philip Hadden was engaged for several years in transport- riding—that is, in carrying goods on ox waggons from Durban or Maritzburg to various points in the interior. A difficulty such as had more than once confronted him in the course of his career, led to his temporary abandonment of this means of earning a livelihood. On arriving at the little frontier town of Utrecht in the Transvaal, in charge of two waggon loads of mixed goods consigned to a storekeeper there, it was discovered that out of six cases of brandy five were missing from his waggon. Hadden explained the matter by throwing the blame upon his Kaffir "boys," but the storekeeper, a rough-tongued man, openly called him a thief and refused to pay the freight on any of the load. From words the two men came to blows, knives were drawn, and before anybody could interfere the storekeeper received a nasty wound in his side. That night, without waiting till the matter could be inquired into by the landdrost or magistrate, Hadden slipped away, and trekked back into Natal as quickly as his oxen would travel. Feeling that even here he was not safe, he left one of his waggons at Newcastle, loaded up the other with Kaffir goods—such as blankets, calico, and hardware—and crossed into Zululand, where in those days no sheriff's officer would be likely to follow him.

Being well acquainted with the language and customs of the natives, he did good trade with them, and soon found himself possessed of some cash and a small herd of cattle, which he received in exchange for his wares. Meanwhile news reached him that the man whom he had injured still vowed vengeance against him, and was in communication with the authorities in Natal. These reasons making his return to civilisation undesirable for the moment, and further business being impossible until he could receive a fresh supply of trade stuff, Hadden like a wise man turned his thoughts to pleasure. Sending his cattle and waggon over the border to be left in charge of a native headman with whom he was friendly, he went on foot to Ulundi to obtain permission from the king, Cetywayo, to hunt game in his country. Somewhat to his surprise, the Indunas or headmen, received him courteously—for Hadden's visit took place within a few months of the outbreak of the Zulu war in 1878, when Cetywayo was already showing unfriendliness to the English traders and others, though why the king did so they knew not.

On the occasion of his first and last interview with Cetywayo, Hadden got a hint of the reason. It happened thus. On the second morning after his arrival at the royal kraal, a messenger came to inform him that "the Elephant whose tread shook the earth" had signified that it was his pleasure to see him. Accordingly he was led through the thousands of huts and across the Great Place to the little enclosure where Cetywayo, a royal-looking Zulu seated on a stool, and wearing a kaross of leopard skins, was holding an indaba, or conference, surrounded by his counsellors. The Induna who had conducted him to the august presence went down upon his hands and knees, and, uttering the royal salute of Bayéte, crawled forward to announce that the white man was waiting.

"Let him wait," said the king angrily; and, turning, he continued the discussion with his counsellors.

Now, as has been said, Hadden thoroughly understood Zulu; and, when from time to time the king raised his voice, some of the words he spoke reached his ear.

"What!" Cetywayo said, to a wizened and aged man who seemed to be pleading with him earnestly; "am I a dog that these white hyenas should hunt me thus? Is not the land mine, and was it not my father's before me? Are not the people mine to save or to slay? I tell you that I will stamp out these little white men; my impis shall eat them up. I have said!"

Again the withered aged man interposed, evidently in the character of a peacemaker. Hadden could not hear his talk, but he rose and pointed towards the sea, while from his expressive gestures and sorrowful mien, he seemed to be prophesying disaster should a certain course of action be followed.

For a while the king listened to him, then he sprang from his seat, his eyes literally ablaze with rage.

"Hearken," he cried to the counsellor; "I have guessed it for long, and now I am sure of it. You are a traitor. You are Sompseu's[*] dog, and the dog of the Natal Government, and I will not keep another man's dog to bite me in my own house. Take him away!"

[*] Sir Theophilus Shepstone's.

A slight involuntary murmur rose from the ring of indunas, but the old man never flinched, not even when the soldiers, who presently would murder him, came and seized him roughly. For a few seconds, perhaps five, he covered his face with the corner of the kaross he wore, then he looked up and spoke to the king in a clear voice.

"O King," he said, "I am a very old man; as a youth I served under Chaka the Lion, and I heard his dying prophecy of the coming of the white man. Then the white men came, and I fought for Dingaan at the battle of the Blood River. They slew Dingaan, and for many years I was the counsellor of Panda, your father. I stood by you, O King, at the battle of the Tugela, when its grey waters were turned to red with the blood of Umbulazi your brother, and of the tens of thousands of his people. Afterwards I became your counsellor, O King, and I was with you when Sompseu set the crown upon your head and you made promises to Sompseu—promises that you have not kept. Now you are weary of me, and it is well; for I am very old, and doubtless my talk is foolish, as it chances to the old. Yet I think that the prophecy of Chaka, your great-uncle, will come true, and that the white men will prevail against you and that through them you shall find your death. I would that I might have stood in one more battle and fought for you, O King, since fight you will, but the end which you choose is for me the best end. Sleep in peace, O King, and farewell. Bayéte!"[*]

[*] The royal salute of the Zulus.

For a space there was silence, a silence of expectation while men waited to hear the tyrant reverse his judgment. But it did not please him to be merciful, or the needs of policy outweighed his pity.

"Take him away," he repeated. Then, with a slow smile on his face and one word, "Good-night," upon his lips, supported by the arm of a soldier, the old warrior and statesman shuffled forth to the place of death.

Hadden watched and listened in amazement not unmixed with fear. "If he treats his own servants like this, what will happen to me?" he reflected. "We English must have fallen out of favour since I left Natal. I wonder whether he means to make war on us or what? If so, this isn't my place."

Just then the king, who had been gazing moodily at the ground, chanced to look up. "Bring the stranger here," he said.

Hadden heard him, and coming forward offered Cetywayo his hand in as cool and nonchalant a manner as he could command.

Somewhat to his surprise it was accepted. "At least, White Man," said the king, glancing at his visitor's tall spare form and cleanly cut face, "you are no 'umfagozan' (low fellow); you are of the blood of chiefs."

"Yes, King," answered Hadden, with a little sigh, "I am of the blood of chiefs."

"What do you want in my country, White Man?"

"Very little, King. I have been trading here, as I daresay you have heard, and have sold all my goods. Now I ask your leave to hunt buffalo, and other big game, for a while before I return to Natal."

"I cannot grant it," answered Cetywayo, "you are a spy sent by Sompseu, or by the Queen's Induna in Natal. Get you gone."

"Indeed," said Hadden, with a shrug of his shoulders; "then I hope that Sompseu, or the Queen's Induna, or both of them, will pay me when I return to my own country. Meanwhile I will obey you because I must, but I should first like to make you a present."

"What present?" asked the king. "I want no presents. We are rich here, White Man."

"So be it, King. It was nothing worthy of your taking, only a rifle."

"A rifle, White Man? Where is it?"

"Without. I would have brought it, but your servants told me that it is death to come armed before the 'Elephant who shakes the Earth.'"

Cetywayo frowned, for the note of sarcasm did not escape his quick ear.

"Let this white man's offering be brought; I will consider the thing."

Instantly the Induna who had accompanied Hadden darted to the gateway, running with his body bent so low that it seemed as though at every step he must fall upon his face. Presently he returned with the weapon in his hand and presented it to the king, holding it so that the muzzle was pointed straight at the royal breast.

"I crave leave to say, O Elephant," remarked Hadden in a drawling voice, "that it might be well to command your servant to lift the mouth of that gun from your heart."

"Why?" asked the king.

"Only because it is loaded, and at full cock, O Elephant, who probably desires to continue to shake the Earth."

At these words the "Elephant" uttered a sharp exclamation, and rolled from his stool in a most unkingly manner, whilst the terrified Induna, springing backwards, contrived to touch the trigger of the rifle and discharge a bullet through the exact spot that a second before had been occupied by his monarch's head.

"Let him be taken away," shouted the incensed king from the ground, but long before the words had passed his lips the Induna, with a cry that the gun was bewitched, had cast it down and fled at full speed through the gate.

"He has already taken himself away," suggested Hadden, while the audience tittered. "No, King, do not touch it rashly; it is a repeating rifle. Look—" and lifting the Winchester, he fired the four remaining shots in quick succession into the air, striking the top of a tree at which he aimed with every one of them.

"Wow, it is wonderful!" said the company in astonishment.

"Has the thing finished?" asked the king.

"For the present it has," answered Hadden. "Look at it."

Cetywayo took the repeater in his hand, and examined it with caution, swinging the muzzle horizontally in an exact line with the stomachs of some of his most eminent Indunas, who shrank to this side and that as the barrel was brought to bear on them.

"See what cowards they are, White Man," said the king with indignation; "they fear lest there should be another bullet in this gun."

"Yes," answered Hadden, "they are cowards indeed. I believe that if they were seated on stools they would tumble off them just as it chanced to your Majesty to do just now."

"Do you understand the making of guns, White Man?" asked the king hastily, while the Indunas one and all turned their heads, and contemplated the fence behind them.

"No, King, I cannot make guns, but I can mend them."

"If I paid you well, White Man, would you stop here at my kraal, and mend guns for me?" asked Cetywayo anxiously.

"It might depend on the pay," answered Hadden; "but for awhile I am tired of work, and wish to rest. If the king gives me the permission to hunt for which I asked, and men to go with me, then when I return perhaps we can bargain on the matter. If not, I will bid the king farewell, and journey to Natal."

"In order to make report of what he has seen and learned here," muttered Cetywayo.

At this moment the talk was interrupted, for the soldiers who had led away the old Induna returned at speed, and prostrated themselves before the king.

"Is he dead?" he asked.

"He has travelled the king's bridge," they answered grimly; "he died singing a song of praise of the king."

"Good," said Cetywayo, "that stone shall hurt my feet no more. Go, tell the tale of its casting away to Sompseu and to the Queen's Induna in Natal," he added with bitter emphasis.

"Baba! Hear our Father speak. Listen to the rumbling of the Elephant," said the Indunas taking the point, while one bolder than the rest added: "Soon we will tell them another tale, the white Talking Ones, a red tale, a tale of spears, and the regiments shall sing it in their ears."

At the words an enthusiasm caught hold of the listeners, as the sudden flame catches hold of dry grass. They sprang up, for the most of them were seated on their haunches, and stamping their feet upon the ground in unison, repeated:—

Indaba ibomwu—indaba ye mikonto
Lizo dunyiswa nge impi ndhlebeni yaho.

(A red tale! A red tale! A tale of spears,
And the impis shall sing it in their ears.)

One of them, indeed, a great fierce-faced fellow, drew near to Hadden and shaking his fist before his eyes—fortunately being in the royal presence he had no assegai—shouted the sentences at him.

The king saw that the fire he had lit was burning too fiercely.

"Silence," he thundered in the deep voice for which he was remarkable, and instantly each man became as if he were turned to stone, only the echoes still answered back: "And the impis shall sing it in their ears—in their ears."

"I am growing certain that this is no place for me," thought Hadden; "if that scoundrel had been armed he might have temporarily forgotten himself. Hullo! who's this?"

Just then there appeared through the gate of the fence a splendid specimen of the Zulu race. The man, who was about thirty-five years of age, was arrayed in a full war dress of a captain of the Umcityu regiment. From the circlet of otter skin on his brow rose his crest of plumes, round his middle, arms and knees hung the long fringes of black oxtails, and in one hand he bore a little dancing shield, also black in colour. The other was empty, since he might not appear before the king bearing arms. In countenance the man was handsome, and though just now they betrayed some anxiety, his eyes were genial and honest, and his mouth sensitive. In height he must have measured six foot two inches, yet he did not strike the observer as being tall, perhaps because of his width of chest and the solidity of his limbs, that were in curious contrast to the delicate and almost womanish hands and feet which so often mark the Zulu of noble blood. In short the man was what he seemed to be, a savage gentleman of birth, dignity and courage.

In company with him was another man plainly dressed in a moocha and a blanket, whose grizzled hair showed him to be over fifty years of age. His face also was pleasant and even refined, but the eyes were timorous, and the mouth lacked character.

"Who are these?" asked the king.

The two men fell on their knees before him, and bowed till their foreheads touched the ground—the while giving him his sibonga or titles of praise.

"Speak," he said impatiently.

"O King," said the young warrior, seating himself Zulu fashion, "I am Nahoon, the son of Zomba, a captain of the Umcityu, and this is my uncle Umgona, the brother of one of my mothers, my father's youngest wife."

Cetywayo frowned. "What do you here away from your regiment, Nahoon?"

"May it please the king, I have leave of absence from the head captains, and I come to ask a boon of the king's bounty."

"Be swift, then, Nahoon."

"It is this, O King," said the captain with some embarrassment: "A while ago the king was pleased to make a keshla of me because of certain service that I did out yonder—" and he touched the black ring which he wore in the hair of his head. "Being now a ringed man and a captain, I crave the right of a man at the hands of the king—the right to marry."

"Right? Speak more humbly, son of Zomba; my soldiers and my cattle have no rights."

Nahoon bit his lip, for he had made a serious mistake.

"Pardon, O King. The matter stands thus: My uncle Umgona here has a fair daughter named Nanea, whom I desire to wife, and who desires me to husband. Awaiting the king's leave I am betrothed to her and in earnest of it I have paid to Umgona a lobola of fifteen head of cattle, cows and calves together. But Umgona has a powerful neighbour, an old chief named Maputa, the warden of the Crocodile Drift, who doubtless is known to the king, and this chief also seeks Nanea in marriage and harries Umgona, threatening him with many evils if he will not give the girl to him. But Umgona's heart is white towards me, and towards Maputa it is black, therefore together we come to crave this boon of the king."

"It is so; he speaks the truth," said Umgona.

"Cease," answered Cetywayo angrily. "Is this a time that my soldiers should seek wives in marriage, wives to turn their hearts to water? Know that but yesterday for this crime I commanded that twenty girls who had dared without my leave to marry men of the Undi regiment, should be strangled and their bodies laid upon the cross-roads and with them the bodies of their fathers, that all might know their sin and be warned thereby. Ay, Umgona, it is well for you and for your daughter that you sought my word before she was given in marriage to this man. Now this is my award: I refuse your prayer, Nahoon, and since you, Umgona, are troubled with one whom you would not take as son-in-law, the old chief Maputa, I will free you from his importunity. The girl, says Nahoon, is fair—good, I myself will be gracious to her, and she shall be numbered among the wives of the royal house. Within thirty days from now, in the week of the next new moon, let her be delivered to the Sigodhla, the royal house of the women, and with her those cattle, the cows and the calves together, that Nahoon has given you, of which I fine him because he has dared to think of marriage without the leave of the king."

Chapter II

The Bee Prophesies

"'A Daniel come to judgment' indeed," reflected Hadden, who had been watching this savage comedy with interest; "our love-sick friend has got more than he bargained for. Well, that comes of appealing to Cæsar," and he turned to look at the two suppliants.

The old man, Umgona, merely started, then began to pour out sentences of conventional thanks and praise to the king for his goodness and condescension. Cetywayo listened to his talk in silence, and when he had done answered by reminding him tersely that if Nanea did not appear at the date named, both she and he, her father, would in due course certainly decorate a cross-road in their own immediate neighbourhood.

The captain, Nahoon, afforded a more curious study. As the fatal words crossed the king's lips, his face took an expression of absolute astonishment, which was presently replaced by one of fury—the just fury of a man who suddenly has suffered an unutterable wrong. His whole frame quivered, the veins stood out in knots on his neck and forehead, and his fingers closed convulsively as though they were grasping the handle of a spear. Presently the rage passed away—for as well might a man be wroth with fate as with a Zulu despot—to be succeeded by a look of the most hopeless misery. The proud dark eyes grew dull, the copper-coloured face sank in and turned ashen, the mouth drooped, and down one corner of it there trickled a little line of blood springing from the lip bitten through in the effort to keep silence. Lifting his hand in salute to the king, the great man rose and staggered rather than walked towards the gate.

As he reached it, the voice of Cetywayo commanded him to stop. "Stay," he said, "I have a service for you, Nahoon, that shall drive out of your head these thoughts of wives and marriage. You see this white man here; he is my guest, and would hunt buffalo and big game in the bush country. I put him in your charge; take men with you, and see that he comes to no hurt. So also that you bring him before me within a month, or your life shall answer for it. Let him be here at my royal kraal in the first week of the new moon—when Nanea comes—and then I will tell you whether or no I agree with you that she is fair. Go now, my child, and you, White Man, go also; those who are to accompany you shall be with you at the dawn. Farewell, but remember we meet again at the new moon, when we will settle what pay you shall receive as keeper of my guns. Do not fail me, White Man, or I shall send after you, and my messengers are sometimes rough."

"This means that I am a prisoner," thought Hadden, "but it will go hard if I cannot manage to give them the slip somehow. I don't intend to stay in this country if war is declared, to be pounded into mouti (medicine), or have my eyes put out, or any little joke of that sort."

Ten days had passed, and one evening Hadden and his escort were encamped in a wild stretch of mountainous country lying between the Blood and Unvunyana Rivers, not more than eight miles from that "Place of the Little Hand" which within a few weeks was to become famous throughout the world by its native name of Isandhlwana. For three days they had been tracking the spoor of a small herd of buffalo that still inhabited the district, but as yet they had not come up with them. The Zulu hunters had suggested that they should follow the Unvunyana down towards the sea where game was more plentiful, but this neither Hadden, nor the captain, Nahoon, had been anxious to do, for reasons which each of them kept secret to himself. Hadden's object was to work gradually down to the Buffalo River across which he hoped to effect a retreat into Natal. That of Nahoon was to linger in the neighbourhood of the kraal of Umgona, which was situated not very far from their present camping place, in the vague hope that he might find an opportunity of speaking with or at least of seeing Nanea, the girl to whom he was affianced, who within a few weeks must be taken from him, and given over to the king.

A more eerie-looking spot than that where they were encamped Hadden had never seen. Behind them lay a tract of land—half-swamp and half- bush—in which the buffalo were supposed to be hiding. Beyond, in lonely grandeur, rose the mountain of Isandhlwana, while in front was an amphitheatre of the most gloomy forest, ringed round in the distance by sheer-sided hills. Into this forest there ran a river which drained the swamp, placidly enough upon the level. But it was not always level, for within three hundred yards of them it dashed suddenly over a precipice, of no great height but very steep, falling into a boiling rock-bound pool that the light of the sun never seemed to reach.

"What is the name of that forest, Nahoon?" asked Hadden.

"It is named Emagudu, The Home of the Dead," the Zulu replied absently, for he was looking towards the kraal of Nanea, which was situated at an hour's walk away over the ridge to the right.

"The Home of the Dead! Why?"

"Because the dead live there, those whom we name the Esemkofu, the Speechless Ones, and with them other Spirits, the Amahlosi, from whom the breath of life has passed away, and who yet live on."

"Indeed," said Hadden, "and have you ever seen these ghosts?"

"Am I mad that I should go to look for them, White Man? Only the dead enter that forest, and it is on the borders of it that our people make offerings to the dead."

Followed by Nahoon, Hadden walked to the edge of the cliff and looked over it. To the left lay the deep and dreadful-looking pool, while close to the bank of it, placed upon a narrow strip of turf between the cliff and the commencement of the forest, was a hut.

"Who lives there?" asked Hadden.

"The great Isanusi—she who is named Inyanga or Doctoress; she who is named Inyosi (the Bee), because she gathers wisdom from the dead who grow in the forest."

"Do you think that she could gather enough wisdom to tell me whether I am going to kill any buffalo, Nahoon?"

"Mayhap, White Man, but," he added with a little smile, "those who visit the Bee's hive may hear nothing, or they may hear more than they wish for. The words of that Bee have a sting."

"Good; I will see if she can sting me."

"So be it," said Nahoon; and turning, he led the way along the cliff till he reached a native path which zig-zagged down its face.

By this path they climbed till they came to the sward at the foot of the descent, and walked up it to the hut which was surrounded by a low fence of reeds, enclosing a small court-yard paved with ant-heap earth beaten hard and polished. In this court-yard sat the Bee, her stool being placed almost at the mouth of the round opening that served as a doorway to the hut. At first all that Hadden could see of her, crouched as she was in the shadow, was a huddled shape wrapped round with a greasy and tattered catskin kaross, above the edge of which appeared two eyes, fierce and quick as those of a leopard. At her feet smouldered a little fire, and ranged around it in a semi-circle were a number of human skulls, placed in pairs as though they were talking together, whilst other bones, to all appearance also human, were festooned about the hut and the fence of the courtyard.

"I see that the old lady is set up with the usual properties," thought Hadden, but he said nothing.

Nor did the witch-doctoress say anything; she only fixed her beady eyes upon his face. Hadden returned the compliment, staring at her with all his might, till suddenly he became aware that he was vanquished in this curious duel. His brain grew confused, and to his fancy it seemed that the woman before him had shifted shape into the likeness of colossal and horrid spider sitting at the mouth of her trap, and that these bones were the relics of her victims.

"Why do you not speak, White Man?" she said at last in a slow clear voice. "Well, there is no need, since I can read your thoughts. You are thinking that I who am called the Bee should be better named the

Spider. Have no fear; I did not kill these men. What would it profit me when the dead are so many? I suck the souls of men, not their bodies, White Man. It is their living hearts I love to look on, for therein I read much and thereby I grow wise. Now what would you of the Bee, White Man, the Bee that labours in this Garden of Death, and—what brings you here, son of Zomba? Why are you not with the Umcityu now that they doctor themselves for the great war—the last war—the war of the white and the black—or if you have no stomach for fighting, why are you not at the side of Nanea the tall, Nanea the fair?"

Nahoon made no answer, but Hadden said:—

"A small thing, mother. I would know if I shall prosper in my hunting."

"In your hunting, White Man; what hunting? The hunting of game, of money, or of women? Well, one of them, for a-hunting you must ever be; that is your nature, to hunt and be hunted. Tell me now, how goes the wound of that trader who tasted of your steel yonder in the town of the Maboon (Boers)? No need to answer, White Man, but what fee, Chief, for the poor witch-doctoress whose skill you seek," she added in a whining voice. "Surely you would not that an old woman should work without a fee?"

"I have none to offer you, mother, so I will be going," said Hadden, who began to feel himself satisfied with this display of the Bee's powers of observation and thought-reading.

"Nay," she answered with an unpleasant laugh, "would you ask a question, and not wait for the answer? I will take no fee from you at present, White Man; you shall pay me later on when we meet again," and once more she laughed. "Let me look in your face, let me look in your face," she continued, rising and standing before him.

Then of a sudden Hadden felt something cold at the back of his neck, and the next instant the Bee had sprung from him, holding between her thumb and finger a curl of dark hair which she had cut from his head. The action was so instantaneous that he had neither time to avoid nor to resent it, but stood still staring at her stupidly.

"That is all I need," she cried, "for like my heart my magic is white. Stay—son of Zomba, give me also of your hair, for those who visit the Bee must listen to her humming."

Nahoon obeyed, cutting a little lock from his head with the sharp edge of his assegai, though it was very evident that he did this not because he wished to do so, but because he feared to refuse.

Then the Bee slipped back her kaross, and stood bending over the fire before them, into which she threw herbs taken from a pouch that was bound about her middle. She was still a finely-shaped woman, and she wore none of the abominations which Hadden had been accustomed to see upon the persons of witch-doctoresses. About her neck, however, was a curious ornament, a small live snake, red and grey in hue, which her visitors recognised as one of the most deadly to be found in that part of the country. It is not unusual for Bantu witch-doctors thus to decorate themselves with snakes, though whether or not their fangs have first been extracted no one seems to know.

Presently the herbs began to smoulder, and the smoke of them rose up in a thin, straight stream, that, striking upon the face of the Bee, clung about her head enveloping it as though with a strange blue veil. Then of a sudden she stretched out her hands, and let fall the two locks of hair upon the burning herbs, where they writhed themselves to ashes like things alive. Next she opened her mouth, and began to draw the fumes of the hair and herbs into her lungs in great gulps; while the snake, feeling the influence of the medicine, hissed and, uncoiling itself from about her neck, crept upwards and took refuge among the black saccaboola feathers of her head-dress.

Soon the vapours began to do their work; she swayed to and fro muttering, then sank back against the hut, upon the straw of which her head rested. Now the Bee's face was turned upwards towards the light, and it was ghastly to behold, for it had become blue in colour, and the open eyes were sunken like the eyes of one dead, whilst above her forehead the red snake wavered and hissed, reminding Hadden of the Uraeus crest on the brow of statues of Egyptian kings. For ten seconds or more she remained thus, then she spoke in a hollow and unnatural voice:—

"O Black Heart and body that is white and beautiful, I look into your heart, and it is black as blood, and it shall be black with blood. Beautiful white body with black heart, you shall find your game and hunt it, and it shall lead you into the House of the Homeless, into the Home of the Dead, and it shall be shaped as a bull, it shall be shaped as a tiger, it shall be shaped as a woman whom kings and waters cannot harm. Beautiful white body and black heart, you shall be paid your wages, money for money, and blow for blow. Think of my word when the spotted cat purrs above your breast; think of it when the battle roars about you; think of it when you grasp your great reward, and for the last time stand face to face with the ghost of the dead in the Home of the Dead.

"O White Heart and black body, I look into your heart and it is white as milk, and the milk of innocence shall save it. Fool, why do you strike that blow? Let him be who is loved of the tiger, and whose love is as the love of a tiger. Ah! what face is that in the battle? Follow it, follow it, O swift of foot; but follow warily, for the tongue that has lied will never plead for mercy, and the hand that can betray is strong in war. White Heart, what is death? In death life lives, and among the dead you shall find the life you lost, for there awaits you she whom kings and waters cannot harm."

As the Bee spoke, by degrees her voice sank lower and lower till it was almost inaudible. Then it ceased altogether and she seemed to pass from trance to sleep. Hadden, who had been listening to her with an amused and cynical smile, now laughed aloud.

"Why do you laugh, White Man?" asked Nahoon angrily.

"I laugh at my own folly in wasting time listening to the nonsense of that lying fraud."

"It is no nonsense, White Man."

"Indeed? Then will you tell me what it means?"

"I cannot tell you what it means yet, but her words have to do with a woman and a leopard, and with your fate and my fate."

Hadden shrugged his shoulders, not thinking the matter worth further argument, and at that moment the Bee woke up shivering, drew the red snake from her head-dress and coiling it about her throat wrapped herself again in the greasy kaross.

"Are you satisfied with my wisdom, Inkoos?" she asked of Hadden.

"I am satisfied that you are one of the cleverest cheats in Zululand, mother," he answered coolly. "Now, what is there to pay?"

The Bee took no offence at this rude speech, though for a second or two the look in her eyes grew strangely like that which they had seen in those of the snake when the fumes of the fire made it angry.

"If the white lord says I am a cheat, it must be so," she answered, "for he of all men should be able to discern a cheat. I have said that I ask no fee;—yes, give me a little tobacco from your pouch."

Hadden opened the bag of antelope hide and drawing some tobacco from it, gave it to her. In taking it she clasped his hand and examined the gold ring that was upon the third finger, a ring fashioned like a snake with two little rubies set in the head to represent the eyes.

"I wear a snake about my neck, and you wear one upon your hand, Inkoos. I should like to have this ring to wear upon my hand, so that the snake about my neck may be less lonely there."

"Then I am afraid you will have to wait till I am dead," said Hadden.

"Yes, yes," she answered in a pleased voice, "it is a good word. I will wait till you are dead and then I will take the ring, and none can say that I have stolen it, for Nahoon there will bear me witness that you gave me permission to do so."

For the first time Hadden started, since there was something about the Bee's tone that jarred upon him. Had she addressed him in her professional manner, he would have thought nothing of it; but in her cupidity she had become natural, and it was evident that she spoke from conviction, believing her own words.

She saw him start, and instantly changed her note.

"Let the white lord forgive the jest of a poor old witch-doctoress," she said in a whining voice. "I have so much to do with Death that his name leaps to my lips," and she glanced first at the circle of skulls about her, then towards the waterfall that fed the gloomy pool upon whose banks her hut was placed.

"Look," she said simply.

Following the line of her outstretched hand Hadden's eyes fell upon two withered mimosa trees which grew over the fall almost at right angles to its rocky edge. These trees were joined together by a rude platform made of logs of wood lashed down with riems of hide. Upon this platform stood three figures; notwithstanding the distance and the spray of the fall, he could see that they were those of two men and a girl, for their shapes stood out distinctly against the fiery red of the sunset sky. One instant there were three, the next there were two—for the girl had gone, and something dark rushing down the face of the fall, struck the surface of the pool with a heavy thud, while a faint and piteous cry broke upon his ear.

"What is the meaning of that?" he asked, horrified and amazed.

"Nothing," answered the Bee with a laugh. "Do you not know, then, that this is the place where faithless women, or girls who have loved without the leave of the king, are brought to meet their death, and with them their accomplices. Oh! they die here thus each day, and I watch them die and keep the count of the number of them," and drawing a tally-stick from the thatch of the hut, she took a knife and added a notch to the many that appeared upon it, looking at Nahoon the while with a half-questioning, half-warning gaze.

"Yes, yes, it is a place of death," she muttered. "Up yonder the quick die day by day and down there"—and she pointed along the course of the river beyond the pool to where the forest began some two hundred yards from her hut—"the ghosts of them have their home. Listen!"

As she spoke, a sound reached their ears that seemed to swell from the dim skirts of the forests, a peculiar and unholy sound which it is impossible to define more accurately than by saying that it seemed beastlike, and almost inarticulate.

"Listen," repeated the Bee, "they are merry yonder."

"Who?" asked Hadden; "the baboons?"

"No, Inkoos, the Amatongo—the ghosts that welcome her who has just become of their number."

"Ghosts," said Hadden roughly, for he was angry at his own tremors, "I should like to see those ghosts. Do you think that I have never heard a troop of monkeys in the bush before, mother? Come, Nahoon, let us be going while there is light to climb the cliff. Farewell."

"Farewell Inkoos, and doubt not that your wish will be fulfilled. Go in peace Inkoos—to sleep in peace."

Chapter III

The End of the Hunt

The prayer of the Bee notwithstanding, Philip Hadden slept ill that night. He felt in the best of health, and his conscience was not troubling him more than usual, but rest he could not. Whenever he closed his eyes, his mind conjured up a picture of the grim witch- doctoress, so strangely named the Bee, and the sound of her evil- omened words as he had heard them that afternoon. He was neither a superstitious nor a timid man, and any supernatural beliefs that might linger in his mind were, to say the least of it, dormant. But do what he might, he could not shake off a certain eerie sensation of fear, lest there should be some grains of truth in the prophesyings of this hag. What if it were a fact that he was near his death, and that the heart which beat so strongly in his breast must soon be still for ever—no, he would not think of it. This gloomy place, and the dreadful sight which he saw that day, had upset his nerves. The domestic customs of these Zulus were not pleasant, and for his part he was determined to be clear of them so soon as he was able to escape the country.

In fact, if he could in any way manage it, it was his intention to make a dash for the border on the following night. To do this with a good prospect of success, however, it was necessary that he should kill a buffalo, or some other head of game. Then, as he knew well, the hunters with him would feast upon meat until they could scarcely stir, and that would be his opportunity. Nahoon, however, might not succumb to this temptation; therefore he must trust to luck to be rid of him. If it came to the worst, he could put a bullet through him, which he considered he would be justified in doing, seeing that in reality the man was his jailor. Should this necessity arise, he felt indeed that he could face it without undue compunction, for in truth he disliked Nahoon; at times he even hated him. Their natures were antagonistic, and he knew that the great Zulu distrusted and looked down upon him, and to be looked down upon by a savage "nigger" was more than his pride could stomach.

At the first break of dawn Hadden rose and roused his escort, who were still stretched in sleep around the dying fire, each man wrapped in his kaross or blanket. Nahoon stood up and shook himself, looking gigantic in the shadows of the morning.

"What is your will, Umlungu (white man), that you are up before the sun?"

"My will, Muntumpofu (yellow man), is to hunt buffalo," answered Hadden coolly. It irritated him that this savage should give him no title of any sort.

"Your pardon," said the Zulu reading his thoughts, "but I cannot call you Inkoos because you are not my chief, or any man's; still if the title 'white man' offends you, we will give you a name."

"As you wish," answered Hadden briefly.

Accordingly they gave him a name, Inhlizin-mgama, by which he was known among them thereafter, but Hadden was not best pleased when he found that the meaning of those soft-sounding syllables was "Black Heart." That was how the inyanga had addressed him—only she used different words.

An hour later, and they were in the swampy bush country that lay behind the encampment searching for their game. Within a very little while Nahoon held up his hand, then pointed to the ground. Hadden looked; there, pressed deep in the marshy soil, and to all appearance not ten minutes old, was the spoor of a small herd of buffalo.

"I knew that we should find game to-day," whispered Nahoon, "because the Bee said so."

"Curse the Bee," answered Hadden below his breath. "Come on."

For a quarter of an hour or more they followed the spoor through thick reeds, till suddenly Nahoon whistled very softly and touched Hadden's arm. He looked up, and there, about two hundred yards away, feeding on some higher ground among a patch if mimosa trees, were the buffaloes—six of them—an old bull with a splendid head, three cows, a heifer and a calf about four months old. Neither the wind nor the nature of the veldt were favourable for them to stalk the game from their present position, so they made a detour of half a mile and very carefully crept towards them up the wind, slipping from trunk to trunk of the mimosas and when these failed them, crawling on their stomachs under cover of the tall tambuti grass. At last they were within forty yards, and a further advance seemed impracticable; for although he could not smell them, it was evident from his movements that the old bull heard some unusual sound and was growing suspicious. Nearest to Hadden, who alone of the party had a rifle, stood the heifer broadside on—a beautiful shot. Remembering that she would make the best beef, he lifted his Martini, and aiming at her immediately behind the shoulder, gently squeezed the trigger. The rifle exploded, and the heifer fell dead, shot through the heart. Strangely enough the other buffaloes did not at once run away. On the contrary, they seemed puzzled to account for the sudden noise; and, not being able to wind anything, lifted their heads and stared round them.

The pause gave Hadden space to get in a fresh cartridge and to aim again, this time at the old bull. The bullet struck him somewhere in the neck or shoulder, for he came to his knees, but in another second was up and having caught sight of the cloud of smoke he charged straight at it. Because of this smoke, or for some other reason, Hadden did not see him coming, and in consequence would most certainly have been trampled or gored, had not Nahoon sprung forward, at the imminent risk of his own life, and dragged him down behind an ant- heap. A moment more and the great beast had thundered by, taking no further notice of them.

"Forward," said Hadden, and leaving most of the men to cut up the heifer and carry the best of her meat to camp, they started on the blood spoor.

For some hours they followed the bull, till at last they lost the trail on a patch of stony ground thickly covered with bush, and exhausted by the heat, sat down to rest and to eat some biltong or sun-dried flesh which they had with them. They finished their meal, and were preparing to return to the camp, when one of the four Zulus who were with them went to drink at a little stream that ran at a distance of not more than ten paces away. Half a minute later they heard a hideous grunting noise and a splashing of water, and saw the Zulu fly into the air. All the while that they were eating, the wounded buffalo had been lying in wait for them under a thick bush on the banks of the streamlet, knowing—cunning brute that he was—that sooner or later his turn would come. With a shout of consternation they rushed forward to see the bull vanish over the rise before Hadden could get a chance of firing at him, and to find their companion dying, for the great horn had pierced his lung.

"It is not a buffalo, it is a devil," the poor fellow gasped, and expired.

"Devil or not, I mean to kill it," exclaimed Hadden. So leaving the others to carry the body of their comrade to camp, he started on accompanied by Nahoon only. Now the ground was more open and the chase easier, for they sighted their quarry frequently, though they could not come near enough to fire. Presently they travelled down a steep cliff.

"Do you know where we are?" asked Nahoon, pointing to a belt of forest opposite. "That is Emagudu, the Home of the Dead—and look, the bull heads thither."

Hadden glanced round him. It was true; yonder to the left were the Fall, the Pool of Doom, and the hut of the Bee.

"Very well," he answered; "then we must head for it too."

Nahoon halted. "Surely you would not enter there," he exclaimed.

"Surely I will," replied Hadden, "but there is no need for you to do so if you are afraid."

"I am afraid—of ghosts," said the Zulu, "but I will come."

So they crossed the strip of turf, and entered the haunted wood. It was a gloomy place indeed; the great wide-topped trees grew thick there shutting out the sight of the sky; moreover, the air in it which no breeze stirred, was heavy with the exhalations of rotting foliage. There seemed to be no life here and no sound—only now and again a loathsome spotted snake would uncoil itself and glide away, and now and again a heavy rotten bough fell with a crash.

Hadden was too intent upon the buffalo, however, to be much impressed by his surroundings. He only remarked that the light would be bad for shooting, and went on.

They must have penetrated a mile or more into the forest when the sudden increase of blood upon the spoor told them that the bull's wound was proving fatal to him.

"Run now," said Hadden cheerfully.

"Nay, hamba gachle—go softly—" answered Nahoon, "the devil is dying, but he will try to play us another trick before he dies." And he went on peering ahead of him cautiously.

"It is all right here, anyway," said Hadden, pointing to the spoor that ran straight forward printed deep in the marshy ground.

Nahoon did not answer, but stared steadily at the trunks of two trees a few paces in front of them and to their right. "Look," he whispered.

Hadden did so, and at length made out the outline of something brown that was crouched behind the trees.

"He is dead," he exclaimed.

"No," answered Nahoon, "he has come back on his own path and is waiting for us. He knows that we are following his spoor. Now if you stand there, I think that you can shoot him through the back between the tree trunks."

Hadden knelt down, and aiming very carefully at a point just below the bull's spine, he fired. There was an awful bellow, and the next instant the brute was up and at them. Nahoon flung his broad spear, which sank deep into its chest, then they fled this way and that. The buffalo stood still for a moment, its fore legs straddled wide and its head down, looking first after the one and then the other, till of a sudden it uttered a low moaning sound and rolled over dead, smashing Nahoon's assegai to fragments as it fell.

"There! he's finished," said Hadden, "and I believe it was your assegai that killed him. Hullo! what's that noise?"

Nahoon listened. In several quarters of the forest, but from how far away it was impossible to tell, there rose a curious sound, as of people calling to each other in fear but in no articulate language. Nahoon shivered.

"It is the Esemkofu," he said, "the ghosts who have no tongue, and who can only wail like infants. Let us be going; this place is bad for mortals."

"And worse for buffaloes," said Hadden, giving the dead bull a kick, "but I suppose that we must leave him here for your friends, the Esemkofu, as we have got meat enough, and can't carry his head."

So they started back towards the open country. As they threaded their way slowly through the tree trunks, a new idea came into Hadden's head. Once out of this forest, he was within an hour's run of the Zulu border, and once over the Zulu border, he would feel a happier man than he did at that moment. As has been said, he had intended to attempt to escape in the darkness, but the plan was risky. All the Zulus might not over-eat themselves and go to sleep, especially after the death of their comrade; Nahoon, who watched him day and night, certainly would not. This was his opportunity—there remained the question of Nahoon.

Well, if it came to the worst, Nahoon must die: it would be easy—he had a loaded rifle, and now that his assegai was gone, Nahoon had only a kerry. He did not wish to kill the man, though it was clear to him, seeing that his own safety was at stake, that he would be amply justified in so doing. Why should he not put it to him—and then be guided by circumstances?

Nahoon was walking across a little open space about ten spaces ahead of him where Hadden could see him very well, whilst he himself was under the shadow of a large tree with low horizontal branches running out from the trunk.

"Nahoon," he said.

The Zulu turned round, and took a step towards him.

"No, do not move, I pray. Stand where you are, or I shall be obliged to shoot you. Listen now: do not be afraid for I shall not fire without warning. I am your prisoner, and you are charged to take me back to the king to be his servant. But I believe that a war is going to break out between your people and mine; and this being so, you will understand that I do not wish to go to Cetywayo's kraal, because I should either come to a violent death there, or my own brothers will believe that I am a traitor and treat me accordingly. The Zulu border is not much more than an hour's journey away—let us say an hour and a half's: I mean to be across it before the moon is up. Now, Nahoon, will you lose me in the forest and give me this hour and a half's start—or will you stop here with that ghost people of whom you talk? Do you understand? No, please do not move."

"I understand you," answered the Zulu, in a perfectly composed voice, "and I think that was a good name which we gave you this morning, though, Black Heart, there is some justice in your words and more wisdom. Your opportunity is good, and one which a man named as you are should not let fall."

"I am glad to find that you take this view of the matter, Nahoon. And now will you be so kind as to lose me, and to promise not to look for me till the moon is up?"

"What do you mean, Black Heart?"

"What I say. Come, I have no time to spare."

"You are a strange man," said the Zulu reflectively. "You heard the king's order to me: would you have me disobey the order of the king?"

"Certainly, I would. You have no reason to love Cetywayo, and it does not matter to you whether or no I return to his kraal to mend guns there. If you think that he will be angry because I am missing, you had better cross the border also; we can go together."

"And leave my father and all my brethren to his vengeance? Black Heart, you do not understand. How can you, being so named? I am a soldier, and the king's word is the king's word. I hoped to have died fighting, but I am the bird in your noose. Come, shoot, or you will not reach the border before moonrise," and he opened his arms and smiled.

"If it must be, so let it be. Farewell, Nahoon, at least you are a brave man, but every one of us must cherish his own life," answered Hadden calmly.

Then with much deliberation he raised his rifle and covered the Zulu's breast.

Already—whilst his victim stood there still smiling, although a twitching of his lips betrayed the natural terrors that no bravery can banish—already his finger was contracting on the trigger, when of a sudden, as instantly as though he had been struck by lightning, Hadden went down backwards, and behold! there stood upon him a great spotted beast that waved its long tail to and fro and glared down into his eyes.

It was a leopard—a tiger as they call it in Africa—which, crouched upon a bough of the tree above, had been unable to resist the temptation of satisfying its savage appetite on the man below. For a second or two there was silence, broken only by the purring, or rather the snoring sound made by the leopard. In those seconds, strangely enough, there sprang up before Hadden's mental vision a picture of the inyanga called Inyosi or the Bee, her death-like head resting against the thatch of the hut, and her death-like lips muttering "think of my word when the great cat purrs above your face."

Then the brute put out its strength. The claws of one paw it drove deep into the muscles of his left thigh, while with another it scratched at his breast, tearing the clothes from it and furrowing the flesh beneath. The sight of the white skin seemed to madden it, and in its fierce desire for blood it drooped its square muzzle and buried its fangs in its victim's shoulder. Next moment there was a sound of running feet and of a club falling heavily. Up reared the leopard with an angry snarl, up till it stood as high as the attacking Zulu. At him it came, striking out savagely and tearing the black man as it had torn the white. Again the kerry fell full on its jaws, and down it went backwards. Before it could rise again, or rather as it was in the act of rising, the heavy knob-stick struck it once more, and with fearful force, this time as it chanced, full on the nape of the neck, and paralysing the brute. It writhed and bit and twisted, throwing up the earth and leaves, while blow after blow was rained upon it, till at length with a convulsive struggle and a stifled roar it lay still—the brains oozing from its shattered skull.

Hadden sat up, the blood running from his wounds.

"You have saved my life, Nahoon," he said faintly, "and I thank you."

"Do not thank me, Black Heart," answered the Zulu, "it was the king's word that I should keep you safely. Still this tiger has been hardly dealt with, for certainly he has saved my life," and lifting the Martini he unloaded the rifle.

At this juncture Hadden swooned away.

Twenty-four hours had gone by when, after what seemed to him to be but a little time of troubled and dreamful sleep, through which he could hear voices without understanding what they said, and feel himself borne he knew not whither, Hadden awoke to find himself lying upon a kaross in a large and beautifully clean Kaffir hut with a bundle of furs for a pillow. There was a bowl of milk at his side and tortured as he was by thirst, he tried to stretch out his arm to lift it to his lips, only to find to his astonishment that his hand fell back to his side like that of a dead man. Looking round the hut impatiently, he found that there was nobody in it to assist him, so he did the only thing which remained for him to do—he lay still. He did not fall asleep, but his eyes closed, and a kind of gentle torpor crept over him, half obscuring his recovered senses. Presently he heard a soft voice speaking; it seemed far away, but he could clearly distinguish the words.

"Black Heart still sleeps," the voice said, "but there is colour in his face; I think that he will wake soon, and find his thoughts again."

"Have no fear, Nanea, he will surely wake, his hurts are not dangerous," answered another voice, that of Nahoon. "He fell heavily with the weight of the tiger on top of him, and that is why his senses have been shaken for so long. He went near to death, but certainly he will not die."

"It would have been a pity if he had died," answered the soft voice, "he is so beautiful; never have I seen a white man who was so beautiful."

"I did not think him beautiful when he stood with his rifle pointed at my heart," answered Nahoon sulkily.

"Well, there is this to be said," she replied, "he wished to escape from Cetywayo, and that is not to be wondered at," and she sighed. "Moreover he asked you to come with him, and it might have been well if you had done so, that is, if you would have taken me with you!"

"How could I have done it, girl?" he asked angrily. "Would you have me set at nothing the order of the king?"

"The king!" she replied raising her voice. "What do you owe to this king? You have served him faithfully, and your reward is that within a few days he will take me from you—me, who should have been your wife, and I must—I must—" And she began to weep softly, adding between her sobs, "if you loved me truly, you would think more of me and of yourself, and less of the Black One and his orders. Oh! let us fly, Nahoon, let us fly to Natal before this spear pierces me."

"Weep not, Nanea," he said; "why do you tear my heart in two between my duty and my love? You know that I am a soldier, and that I must walk the path whereon the king has set my feet. Soon I think I shall be dead, for I seek death, and then it will matter nothing."

"Nothing to you, Nahoon, who are at peace, but to me? Yet, you are right, and I know it, therefore forgive me, who am no warrior, but a woman who must also obey—the will of the king." And she cast her arms about his neck, sobbing her fill upon his breast.

Chapter IV

Nanea

Presently, muttering something that the listener could not catch, Nahoon left Nanea, and crept out of the hut by its bee-hole entrance. Then Hadden opened his eyes and looked round him. The sun was sinking and a ray of its red light streaming through the little opening filled the place with a soft and crimson glow. In the centre of the hut—supporting it—stood a thorn-wood roof-tree coloured black by the smoke of the fire; and against this, the rich light falling full upon her, leaned the girl Nanea—a very picture of gentle despair.

As is occasionally the case among Zulu women, she was beautiful—so beautiful that the sight of her went straight to the white man's heart, for a moment causing the breath to catch in his throat. Her dress was very simple. On her shoulders, hanging open in front, lay a mantle of soft white stuff edged with blue beads, about her middle was a buck-skin moocha, also embroidered with blue beads, while round her forehead and left knee were strips of grey fur, and on her right wrist a shining bangle of copper. Her naked bronze-hued figure was tall and perfect in its proportions; while her face had little in common with that of the ordinary native girl, showing as it did strong traces of the ancestral Arabian or Semitic blood. It was oval in shape, with delicate aquiline features, arched eyebrows, a full mouth, that drooped a little at the corners, tiny ears, behind which the wavy coal-black hair hung down to the shoulders, and the very loveliest pair of dark and liquid eyes that it is possible to imagine.

For a minute or more Nanea stood thus, her sweet face bathed in the sunbeam, while Hadden feasted his eyes upon its beauty. Then sighing heavily, she turned, and seeing that he was awake, started, drew her mantle over her breast and came, or rather glided, towards him.

"The chief is awake," she said in her soft Zulu accents. "Does he need aught?"

"Yes, Lady," he answered; "I need to drink, but alas! I am too weak."

She knelt down beside him, and supporting him with her left arm, with her right held the gourd to his lips.

How it came about Hadden never knew, but before that draught was finished a change passed over him. Whether it was the savage girl's touch, or her strange and fawn-like loveliness, or the tender pity in her eyes, matters not—the issue was the same. She struck some cord in his turbulent uncurbed nature, and of a sudden it was filled full with passion for her—a passion which if, not elevated, at least was real. He did not for a moment mistake the significance of the flood of feeling that surged through his veins. Hadden never shirked facts.

"By Heaven!" he said to himself, "I have fallen in love with a black beauty at first sight—more in love than I have ever been before. It's awkward, but there will be compensations. So much the worse for Nahoon, or for Cetywayo, or for both of them. After all, I can always get rid of her if she becomes a nuisance."

Then, in a fit of renewed weakness, brought about by the turmoil of his blood, he lay back upon the pillow of furs, watching Nanea's face while with a native salve of pounded leaves she busied herself dressing the wounds that the leopard had made.

It almost seemed as though something of what was passing in his mind communicated itself to that of the girl. At least, her hand shook a little at her task, and getting done with it as quickly as she could, she rose from her knees with a courteous "It is finished, Inkoos," and once more took up her position by the roof-tree.

"I thank you, Lady," he said; "your hand is kind."

"You must not call me lady, Inkoos," she answered, "I am no chieftainess, but only the daughter of a headman, Umgona."

"And named Nanea," he said. "Nay, do not be surprised, I have heard of you. Well, Nanea, perhaps you will soon become a chieftainess—up at the king's kraal yonder."

"Alas! and alas!" she said, covering her face with her hands.

"Do not grieve, Nanea, a hedge is never so tall and thick but that it cannot be climbed or crept through."

She let fall her hands and looked at him eagerly, but he did not pursue the subject.

"Tell me, how did I come here, Nanea?"

"Nahoon and his companions carried you, Inkoos."

"Indeed, I begin to be thankful to the leopard that struck me down. Well, Nahoon is a brave man, and he has done me a great service. I trust that I may be able to repay it—to you, Nanea."

This was the first meeting of Nanea and Hadden; but, although she did not seek them, the necessities of his sickness and of the situation brought about many another. Never for a moment did the white man waver in his determination to get into his keeping the native girl who had captivated him, and to attain his end he brought to bear all his powers and charm to detach her from Nahoon, and win her affections for himself. He was no rough wooer, however, but proceeded warily, weaving her about with a web of flattery and attention that must, he thought, produce the desired effect upon her mind. Without a doubt, indeed, it would have done so—for she was but a woman, and an untutored one—had it not been for a simple fact which dominated her whole nature. She loved Nahoon, and there was no room in her heart for any other man, white or black. To Hadden she was courteous and kindly but no more, nor did she appear to notice any of the subtle advances by which he attempted to win a foothold in her heart. For a while this puzzled him, but he remembered that the Zulu women do not usually permit themselves to show feeling towards an undeclared suitor. Therefore it became necessary that he should speak out.

His mind once made up, he had not to wait long for an opportunity. He was now quite recovered from his hurts, and accustomed to walk in the neighbourhood of the kraal. About two hundred yards from Umgona's huts rose a spring, and thither it was Nanea's habit to resort in the evening to bring back drinking-water for the use of her father's household. The path between this spring and the kraal ran through a patch of bush, where on a certain afternoon towards sundown Hadden took his seat under a tree, having first seen Nanea go down to the little stream as was her custom. A quarter of an hour later she reappeared carrying a large gourd upon her head. She wore no garment now except her moocha, for she had but one mantle and was afraid lest the water should splash it. He watched her advancing along the path, her hands resting on her hips, her splendid naked figure outlined against the westering sun, and wondered what excuse he could make to talk with her. As it chanced fortune favoured him, for when she was near him a snake glided across the path in front of the girl's feet, causing her to spring backwards in alarm and overset the gourd of water. He came forward, and picked it up.

"Wait here," he said laughing; "I will bring it to you full."

"Nay, Inkoos," she remonstrated, "that is a woman's work."

"Among my people," he said, "the men love to work for the women," and he started for the spring, leaving her wondering.

Before he reached her again, he regretted his gallantry, for it was necessary to carry the handleless gourd upon his shoulder, and the contents of it spilling over the edge soaked him. Of this, however, he said nothing to Nanea.

"There is your water, Nanea, shall I carry it for you to the kraal?"

"Nay, Inkoos, I thank you, but give it to me, you are weary with its weight."

"Stay awhile, and I will accompany you. Ah! Nanea, I am still weak, and had it not been for you I think that I should be dead."

"It was Nahoon who saved you—not I, Inkoos."

"Nahoon saved my body, but you, Nanea, you alone can save my heart."

"You talk darkly, Inkoos."

"Then I must make my meaning clear, Nanea. I love you."

She opened her brown eyes wide.

"You, a white lord, love me, a Zulu girl? How can that be?"

"I do not know, Nanea, but it is so, and were you not blind you would have seen it. I love you, and I wish to take you to wife."

"Nay, Inkoos, it is impossible. I am already betrothed."

"Ay," he answered, "betrothed to the king."

"No, betrothed to Nahoon."

"But it is the king who will take you within a week; is it not so? And would you not rather that I should take you than the king?"

"It seems to be so, Inkoos, and I would rather go with you than with the king, but most of all I desire to marry Nahoon. It may be that I shall not be able to marry him, but if that is so, at least I will never become one of the king's women."

"How will you prevent it, Nanea?"

"There are waters in which a maid may drown, and trees upon which she can hang," she answered with a quick setting of the mouth.

"That were a pity, Nanea, you are too fair to die."

"Fair or foul, yet I die, Inkoos."

"No, no, come with me—I will find a way—and be my wife," and he put her arm about her waist, and strove to draw her to him.

Without any violence of movement, and with the most perfect dignity, the girl disengaged herself from his embrace.

"You have honoured me, and I thank you, Inkoos," she said quietly, "but you do not understand. I am the wife of Nahoon—I belong to Nahoon; therefore, I cannot look on any other man while Nahoon lives. It is not our custom, Inkoos, for we are not as the white women, but ignorant and simple, and when we vow ourselves to a man, we abide by that vow till death."

"Indeed," said Hadden; "and so now you go to tell Nahoon that I have offered to make you my wife."

"No, Inkoos, why should I tell Nahoon your secrets? I have said 'nay' to you, not 'yea,' therefore he has no right to know," and she stooped to lift the gourd of water.

Hadden considered the situation rapidly, for his repulse only made him the more determined to succeed. Of a sudden under the emergency he conceived a scheme, or rather its rough outline. It was not a nice scheme, and some men might have shrunk from it, but as he had no intention of suffering himself to be defeated by a Zulu girl, he decided—with regret, it is true—that having failed to attain his ends by means which he considered fair, he must resort to others of more doubtful character.

"Nanea," he said, "you are a good and honest woman, and I respect you. As I have told you, I love you also, but if you refuse to listen to me there is nothing more to be said, and after all, perhaps it would be better that you should marry one of your own people. But, Nanea, you will never marry him, for the king will take you; and, if he does not give you to some other man, either you will become one of his 'sisters,' or to be free of him, as you say, you will die. Now hear me, for it is because I love you and wish your welfare that I speak thus. Why do you not escape into Natal, taking Nahoon with you, for there as you know you may live in peace out of reach of the arm of Cetywayo?"

"That is my desire, Inkoos, but Nahoon will not consent. He says that there is to be war between us and you white men, and he will not break the command of the king and desert from his army."

"Then he cannot love you much, Nahoon, and at least you have to think of yourself. Whisper into the ear of your father and fly together, for be sure that Nahoon will soon follow you. Ay! and I myself with fly with you, for I too believe that there must be war, and then a white man in this country will be as a lamb among the eagles."

"If Nahoon will come, I will go, Inkoos, but I cannot fly without Nahoon; it is better I should stay here and kill myself."

"Surely then being so fair and loving him so well, you can teach him to forget his folly and to escape with you. In four days' time we must start for the king's kraal, and if you win over Nahoon, it will be easy for us to turn our faces southwards and across the river that lies between the land of the Amazulu and Natal. For the sake of all of us, but most of all for your own sake, try to do this, Nanea, whom I have loved and whom I now would save. See him and plead with him as you know how, but as yet do not tell him that I dream of flight, for then I should be watched."

"In truth, I will, Inkoos," she answered earnestly, "and oh! I thank you for your goodness. Fear not that I will betray you—first would I die. Farewell."

"Farewell, Nanea," and taking her hand he raised it to his lips.

Late that night, just as Hadden was beginning to prepare himself for sleep, he heard a gentle tapping at the board which closed the entrance to his hut.

"Enter," he said, unfastening the door, and presently by the light of the little lantern that he had with him, he saw Nanea creep into the hut, followed by the great form of Nahoon.

"Inkoos," she said in a whisper when the door was closed again, "I have pleaded with Nahoon, and he has consented to fly; moreover, my father will come also."

"Is it so, Nahoon?" asked Hadden.

"It is so," answered the Zulu, looking down shamefacedly; "to save this girl from the king, and because the love of her eats out my heart, I have bartered away my honour. But I tell you, Nanea, and you, White Man, as I told Umgona just now, that I think no good will come of this flight, and if we are caught or betrayed, we shall be killed every one of us."

"Caught we can scarcely be," broke in Nanea anxiously, "for who could betray us, except the Inkoos here—"

"Which he is not likely to do," said Hadden quietly, "seeing that he desires to escape with you, and that his life is also at stake."

"That is so, Black Heart," said Nahoon, "otherwise I tell you that I should not have trusted you."

Hadden took no notice of this outspoken saying, but until very late that night they sat there together making their plans.

On the following morning Hadden was awakened by sounds of violent altercation. Going out of his hut he found that the disputants were Umgona and a fat and evil-looking Kaffir chief who had arrived at the kraal on a pony. This chief, he soon discovered, was named Maputa, being none other than the man who had sought Nanea in marriage and brought about Nahoon's and Umgona's unfortunate appeal to the king. At present he was engaged in abusing Umgona furiously, charging him with having stolen certain of his oxen and bewitched his cows so that they would not give milk. The alleged theft it was comparatively easy to disprove, but the wizardry remained a matter of argument.

"You are a dog, and a son of a dog," shouted Maputa, shaking his fat fist in the face of the trembling but indignant Umgona. "You promised me your daughter in marriage, then having vowed her to that umfagozan—that low lout of a soldier, Nahoon, the son of Zomba—you went, the two of you, and poisoned the king's ear against me, bringing me into trouble with the king, and now you have bewitched my cattle. Well, wait, I will be even with you, Wizard; wait till you wake up in the cold morning to find your fence red with fire, and the slayers standing outside your gates to eat up you and yours with spears—"

At this juncture Nahoon, who till now had been listening in silence, intervened with effect.

"Good," he said, "we will wait, but not in your company, Chief Maputa. Hamba! (go)—" and seizing the fat old ruffian by the scruff of his neck, he flung him backwards with such violence that he rolled over and over down the little slope.

Hadden laughed, and passed on towards the stream where he proposed to bathe. Just as he reached it, he caught sight of Maputa riding along the footpath, his head-ring covered with mud, his lips purple and his black face livid with rage.

"There goes an angry man," he said to himself. "Now, how would it be—" and he looked upwards like one seeking an inspiration. It seemed to come; perhaps the devil finding it open whispered in his ear, at any rate—in a few seconds his plan was formed, and he was walking through the bush to meet Maputa.

"Go in peace, Chief," he said; "they seem to have treated you roughly up yonder. Having no power to interfere, I came away for I could not bear the sight. It is indeed shameful that an old and venerable man of rank should be struck into the dirt, and beaten by a soldier drunk with beer."

"Shameful, White Man!" gasped Maputa; "your words are true indeed. But wait a while. I, Maputa, will roll that stone over, I will throw that bull upon its back. When next the harvest ripens, this I promise, that neither Nahoon nor Umgona, nor any of his kraal shall be left to gather it."

"And how will you manage that, Maputa?"

"I do not know, but I will find a way. Oh! I tell you, a way shall be found."

Hadden patted the pony's neck meditatively, then leaning forward, he looked the chief in the eyes and said:—

"What will you give me, Maputa, if I show you that way, a sure and certain one, whereby you may be avenged to the death upon Nahoon, whose violence I also have seen, and upon Umgona, whose witchcraft brought sore sickness upon me?"

"What reward do you seek, White Man?" asked Maputa eagerly.

"A little thing, Chief, a thing of no account, only the girl Nanea, to whom as it chances I have taken a fancy."

"I wanted her for myself, White Man, but he who sits at Ulundi has laid his hand upon her."

"That is nothing, Chief; I can arrange with him who 'sits at Ulundi.' It is with you who are great here that I wish to come to terms. Listen: if you grant my desire, not only will I fulfil yours upon your foes, but when the girl is delivered into my hands I will give you this rifle and a hundred rounds of cartridges."

Maputa looked at the sporting Martini, and his eyes glistened.

"It is good," he said; "it is very good. Often have I wished for such a gun that will enable me to shoot game, and to talk with my enemies from far away. Promise it to me, White Man, and you shall take the girl if I can give her to you."

"You swear it, Maputa?"

"I swear it by the head of Chaka, and the spirits of my fathers."

"Good. At dawn on the fourth day from now it is the purpose of Umgona, his daughter Nanea, and Nahoon, to cross the river into Natal by the drift that is called Crocodile Drift, taking their cattle with them and flying from the king. I also shall be of their company, for they know that I have learned their secret, and would murder me if I tried to leave them. Now you who are chief of the border and guardian of that drift, must hide at night with some men among the rocks in the shallows of the drift and await our coming. First Nanea will cross driving the cows and calves, for so it is arranged, and I shall help her; then will follow Umgona and Nahoon with the oxen and heifers. On these two you must fall, killing them and capturing the cattle, and afterwards I will give you the rifle."

"What if the king should ask for the girl, White Man?"

"Then you shall answer that in the uncertain light you did not recognise her and so she slipped away from you; moreover, that at first you feared to seize the girl lest her cries should alarm the men and they should escape you."

"Good, but how can I be sure that you will give me the gun once you are across the river?"

"Thus: before I enter the ford I will lay the rifle and cartridges upon a stone by the bank, telling Nanea that I shall return to fetch them when I have driven over the cattle."

"It is well, White Man; I will not fail you."

So the plot was made, and after some further conversation upon points of detail, the two conspirators shook hands and parted.

"That ought to come off all right," reflected Hadden to himself as he plunged and floated in the waters of the stream, "but somehow I don't quite trust our friend Maputa. It would have been better if I could have relied upon myself to get rid of Nahoon and his respected uncle—a couple of shots would do it in the water. But then that would be murder and murder is unpleasant; whereas the other thing is only the delivery to justice of two base deserters, a laudable action in a military country. Also personal interference upon my part might turn the girl against me; while after Umgona and Nahoon have been wiped out by Maputa, she must accept my escort. Of course there is a risk, but in every walk of life the most cautious have to take risks at times."

As it chanced, Philip Hadden was correct in his suspicions of his coadjutor, Maputa. Even before that worthy chief reached his own kraal, he had come to the conclusion that the white man's plan, though attractive in some ways, was too dangerous, since it was certain that if the girl Nanea escaped, the king would be indignant. Moreover, the men he took with him to do the killing in the drift would suspect something and talk. On the other hand he would earn much credit with his majesty by revealing the plot, saying that he had learned it from the lips of the white hunter, whom Umgona and Nahoon had forced to participate in it, and of whose coveted rifle he must trust to chance to possess himself.

An hour later two discreet messengers were bounding across the plains, bearing words from the Chief Maputa, the Warden of the Border, to the "great Black Elephant" at Ulundi.

Chapter V

The Doom Pool

Fortune showed itself strangely favourable to the plans of Nahoon and Nanea. One of the Zulu captain's perplexities was as to how he should lull the suspicions and evade the vigilance of his own companions, who together with himself had been detailed by the king to assist Hadden in his hunting and to guard against his escape. As it chanced, however, on the day after the incident of the visit of Maputa, a messenger arrived from no less a person than the great military Induna, Tvingwayo ka Marolo, who afterwards commanded the Zulu army at Isandhlwana, ordering these men to return to their regiment, the Umcityu Corps, which was to be placed upon full war footing. Accordingly Nahoon sent them, saying that he himself would follow with Black Heart in the course of a few days, as at present the white man was not sufficiently recovered from his hurts to allow of his travelling fast and far. So the soldiers went, doubting nothing.

Then Umgona gave it out that in obedience to the command of the king he was about to start for Ulundi, taking with him his daughter Nanea to be delivered over into the Sigodhla, and also those fifteen head of cattle that had been lobola'd by Nahoon in consideration of his forthcoming marriage, whereof he had been fined by Cetywayo. Under pretence that they required a change of veldt, the rest of his cattle he sent away in charge of a Basuto herd who knew nothing of their plans, telling him to keep them by the Crocodile Drift, as there the grass was good and sweet.

All preparations being completed, on the third day the party started, heading straight for Ulundi. After they had travelled some miles, however, they left the road and turning sharp to the right, passed unobserved of any through a great stretch of uninhabited bush. Their path now lay not far from the Pool of Doom, which, indeed, was close to Umgona's kraal, and the forest that was called Home of the Dead, but out of sight of these. It was their plan to travel by night, reaching the broken country near the Crocodile Drift on the following morning. Here they proposed to lie hid that day and through the night; then, having first collected the cattle which had preceded them, to cross the river at the break of dawn and escape into Natal. At least this was the plan of his companions; but, as we know, Hadden had another programme, whereon after one last appearance two of the party would play no part.

During that long afternoon's journey Umgona, who knew every inch of the country, walked ahead driving the fifteen cattle and carrying in his hand a long travelling stick of black and white umzimbeet wood, for in truth the old man was in a hurry to reach his journey's end. Next came Nahoon, armed with a broad assegai, but naked except for his moocha and necklet of baboon's teeth, and with him Nanea in her white bead-bordered mantle. Hadden, who brought up the rear, noticed that the girl seemed to be under the spell of an imminent apprehension, for from time to time she clasped her lover's arm, and looking up into his face, addressed him with vehemence, almost with passion.

Curiously enough, the sight touched Hadden, and once or twice he was shaken by so sharp a pang of remorse at the thought of his share in this tragedy, that he cast about in his mind seeking a means to unravel the web of death which he himself had woven. But ever that evil voice was whispering at his ear. It reminded him that he, the white Inkoos, had been refused by this dusky beauty, and that if he found a way to save him, within some few hours she would be the wife of the savage gentleman at her side, the man who had named him Black Heart and who despised him, the man whom he had meant to murder and who immediately repaid his treachery by rescuing him from the jaws of the leopard at the risk of his own life. Moreover, it was a law of Hadden's existence never to deny himself of anything that he desired if it lay within his power to take it—a law which had led him always deeper into sin. In other respects, indeed, it had not carried him far, for in the past he had not desired much, and he had won little; but this particular flower was to his hand, and he would pluck it. If Nahoon stood between him and the flower, so much the worse for Nahoon, and if it should wither in his grasp, so much the worse for the flower; it could always be thrown away. Thus it came about that, not for the first time in his life, Philip Hadden discarded the somewhat spasmodic prickings of conscience and listened to that evil whispering at his ear.

About half-past five o'clock in the afternoon the four refugees passed the stream that a mile or so down fell over the little precipice into the Doom Pool; and, entering a patch of thorn trees on the further side, walked straight into the midst of two-and-twenty soldiers, who were beguiling the tedium of expectancy by the taking of snuff and the smoking of dakka or native hemp. With these soldiers, seated on his pony, for he was too fat to walk, waited the Chief Maputa.

Observing that their expected guests had arrived, the men knocked out the dakka pipe, replaced the snuff boxes in the slits made in the lobes of their ears, and secured the four of them.

"What is the meaning of this, O King's soldiers?" asked Umgona in a quavering voice. "We journey to the kraal of U'Cetywayo; why do you molest us?"

"Indeed. Wherefore then are your faces set towards the south. Does the Black One live in the south? Well, you will journey to another kraal presently," answered the jovial-looking captain of the party with a callous laugh.

"I do not understand," stammered Umgona.

"Then I will explain while you rest," said the captain. "The Chief Maputa yonder sent word to the Black One at Ulundi that he had learned of your intended flight to Natal from the lips of this white man, who had warned him of it. The Black One was angry, and despatched us to catch you and make an end of you. That is all. Come on now, quietly, and let us finish the matter. As the Doom Pool is near, your deaths will be easy."

Nahoon heard the words, and sprang straight at the throat of Hadden; but he did not reach it, for the soldiers pulled him down. Nanea heard them also, and turning, looked the traitor in the eyes; she said nothing, she only looked, but he could never forget that look. The white man for his part was filled with a fiery indignation against Maputa.

"You wicked villain," he gasped, whereat the chief smiled in a sickly fashion, and turned away.

Then they were marched along the banks of the stream till they reached the waterfall that fell into the Pool of Doom.

Hadden was a brave man after his fashion, but his heart quailed as he gazed into that abyss.

"Are you going to throw me in there?" he asked of the Zulu captain in a thick voice.

"You, White Man?" replied the soldier unconcernedly. "No, our orders are to take you to the king, but what he will do with you I do not know. There is to be war between your people and ours, so perhaps he means to pound you into medicine for the use of the witch-doctors, or to peg you over an ant-heap as a warning to other white men."

Hadden received this information in silence, but its effect upon his brain was bracing, for instantly he began to search out some means of escape.

By now the party had halted near the two thorn trees that hung over the waters of the pool.

"Who dives first," asked the captain of the Chief Maputa.

"The old wizard," he replied, nodding at Umgona; "then his daughter after him, and last of all this fellow," and he struck Nahoon in the face with his open hand.

"Come on, Wizard," said the captain, grasping Umgona by the arm, "and let us see how you can swim."

At the words of doom Umgona seemed to recover his self-command, after the fashion of his race.

"No need to lead me, soldier," he said, shaking himself loose, "who am old and ready to die." Then he kissed his daughter at his side, wrung Nahoon by the hand, and turning from Hadden with a gesture of contempt walked out upon the platform that joined the two thorn trunks. Here he stood for a moment looking at the setting sun, then suddenly, and without a sound, he hurled himself into the abyss below and vanished.

"That was a brave one," said the captain with admiration. "Can you spring too, girl, or must we throw you?"

"I can walk my father's path," Nanea answered faintly, "but first I crave leave to say one word. It is true that we were escaping from the king, and therefore by the law we must die; but it was Black Heart here who made the plot, and he who has betrayed us. Would you know why he has betrayed us? Because he sought my favour, and I refused him, and this is the vengeance that he takes—a white man's vengeance."

"Wow!" broke in the chief Maputa, "this pretty one speaks truth, for the white man would have made a bargain with me under which Umgona, the wizard, and Nahoon, the soldier, were to be killed at the Crocodile Drift, and he himself suffered to escape with the girl. I spoke him softly and said 'yes,' and then like a loyal man I reported to the king."

"You hear," sighed Nanea. "Nahoon, fare you well, though presently perhaps we shall be together again. It was I who tempted you from your duty. For my sake you forgot your honour, and I am repaid. Farewell, my husband, it is better to die with you than to enter the house of the king's women," and Nanea stepped on to the platform.

Here, holding to a bough of one of the thorn trees, she turned and addressed Hadden, saying:—

"Black Heart, you seem to have won the day, but me at least you lose and—the sun is not yet set. After sunset comes the night, Black Heart, and in that night I pray that you may wander eternally, and be given to drink of my blood and the blood of Umgona my father, and the blood of Nahoon my husband, who saved your life, and whom you have murdered. Perchance, Black Heart, we may yet meet yonder—in the House of the Dead."

Then uttering a low cry Nanea clasped her hands and sprang upwards and outwards from the platform. The watchers bent their heads forward to look. They saw her rush headlong down the face of the fall to strike the water fifty feet below. A few seconds, and for the last time, they caught sight of her white garment glimmering on the surface of the gloomy pool. Then the shadows and mist-wreaths hid it, and she was gone.

"Now, husband," cried the cheerful voice of the captain, "yonder is your marriage bed, so be swift to follow a bride who is so ready to lead the way. Wow! but you are good people to kill; never have I had to do with any who gave less trouble. You—" and he stopped, for mental agony had done its work, and suddenly Nahoon went mad before his eyes.

With a roar like that of a lion the great man cast off those who held him and seizing one of them round the waist and thigh, he put out all his terrible strength. Lifting him as though he had been an infant, he hurled him over the edge of the cliff to find his death on the rocks of the Pool of Doom. Then crying:—

"Black Heart! your turn, Black Heart the traitor!" he rushed at Hadden, his eyes rolling and foam flying from his lips, as he passed striking the chief Maputa from his horse with a backward blow of his hand. Ill would it have gone with the white man if Nahoon had caught him. But he could not come at him, for the soldiers sprang upon him and notwithstanding his fearful struggles they pulled him to the ground, as at certain festivals the Zulu regiments with their naked hands pull down a bull in the presence of the king.

"Cast him over before he can work more mischief," said a voice. But the captain cried out, "Nay, nay, he is sacred; the fire from Heaven has fallen on his brain, and we may not harm him, else evil would overtake us all. Bind him hand and foot, and bear him tenderly to where he can be cared for. Surely I thought that these evil-doers were giving us too little trouble, and thus it has proved."

So they set themselves to make fast Nahoon's hands and wrists, using as much gentleness as they might, for among the Zulus a lunatic is accounted holy. It was no easy task, and it took time.

Hadden glanced around him, and saw his opportunity. On the ground close beside him lay his rifle, where one of the soldiers had placed it, and about a dozen yards away Maputa's pony was grazing. With a swift movement, he seized the Martini and five seconds later he was on the back of the pony, heading for the Crocodile Drift at a gallop. So quickly indeed did he execute this masterly retreat, that occupied as they all were in binding Nahoon, for half a minute or more none of the soldiers noticed what had happened. Then Maputa chanced to see, and waddled after him to the top of the rise, screaming:—

"The white thief, he has stolen my horse, and the gun too, the gun that he promised to give me."

Hadden, who by this time was a hundred yards away, heard him clearly, and a rage filled his heart. This man had made an open murderer of him; more, he had been the means of robbing him of the girl for whose sake he had dipped his hands in these iniquities. He glanced over his shoulder; Maputa was still running, and alone. Yes, there was time; at any rate he would risk it.

Pulling up the pony with a jerk, he leapt from its back, slipping his arm through the rein with an almost simultaneous movement. As it chanced, and as he had hoped would be the case, the animal was a trained shooting horse, and stood still. Hadden planted his feet firmly on the ground and drawing a deep breath, he cocked the rifle and covered the advancing chief. Now Maputa saw his purpose and with a yell of terror turned to fly. Hadden waited a second to get the sight fair on his broad back, then just as the soldiers appeared above the rise he pressed the trigger. He was a noted shot, and in this instance his skill did not fail him; for, before he heard the bullet tell, Maputa flung his arms wide and plunged to the ground dead.

Three seconds more, and with a savage curse, Hadden had remounted the pony and was riding for his life towards the river, which a while later he crossed in safety.

Chapter VI

The Ghost of the Dead

When Nanea leapt from the dizzy platform that overhung the Pool of Doom, a strange fortune befell her. Close in to the precipice were many jagged rocks, and on these the waters of the fall fell and thundered, bounding from them in spouts of spray into the troubled depths of the foss beyond. It was on these stones that the life was dashed out from the bodies of the wretched victims who were hurled from above. But Nanea, it will be remembered, had not waited to be treated thus, and as it chanced the strong spring with which she had leapt to death carried her clear of the rocks. By a very little she missed the edge of them and striking the deep water head first like some practised diver, she sank down and down till she thought that she would never rise again. Yet she did rise, at the end of the pool in the mouth of the rapid, along which she sped swiftly, carried down by the rush of the water. Fortunately there were no rocks here; and, since she was a skilful swimmer, she escaped the danger of being thrown against the banks.

For a long distance she was borne thus till at length she saw that she was in a forest, for trees cut off the light from the water, and their drooping branches swept its surface. One of these Nanea caught with her hand, and by the help of it she dragged herself from the River of Death whence none had escaped before. Now she stood upon the bank gasping but quite unharmed; there was not a scratch on her body; even her white garment was still fast about her neck.

But though she had suffered no hurt in her terrible voyage, so exhausted was Nanea that she could scarcely stand. Here the gloom was that of night, and shivering with cold she looked helplessly to find some refuge. Close to the water's edge grew an enormous yellow-wood tree, and to this she staggered—thinking to climb it, and seek shelter in its boughs where, as she hoped, she would be safe from wild beasts. Again fortune befriended her, for at a distance of a few feet from the ground there was a great hole in the tree which, she discovered, was hollow. Into this hole she crept, taking her chance of its being the home of snakes or other evil creatures, to find that the interior was wide and warm. It was dry also, for at the bottom of the cavity lay a foot or more of rotten tinder and moss brought there by rats or birds. Upon this tinder she lay down, and covering herself with the moss and leaves soon sank into sleep or stupor.

How long Nanea slept she did not know, but at length she was awakened by a sound as of guttural human voices talking in a language that she could not understand. Rising to her knees she peered out of the hole in the tree. It was night, but the stars shone brilliantly, and their light fell upon an open circle of ground close by the edge of the river. In this circle there burned a great fire, and at a little distance from the fire were gathered eight or ten horrible-looking beings, who appeared to be rejoicing over something that lay upon the ground. They were small in stature, men and women together, but no children, and all of them were nearly naked. Their hair was long and thin, growing down almost to the eyes, their jaws and teeth protruded and the girth of their black bodies was out of all proportion to their height. In their hands they held sticks with sharp stones lashed on to them, or rude hatchet-like knives of the same material.

Now Nanea's heart shrank within her, and she nearly fainted with fear, for she knew that she was in the haunted forest, and without a doubt these were the Esemkofu, the evil ghosts that dwelt therein. Yes, that was what they were, and yet she could not take her eyes off them—the sight of them held her with a horrible fascination. But if they were ghosts, why did they sing and dance like men? Why did they wave those sharp stones aloft, and quarrel and strike each other? And why did they make a fire as men do when they wish to cook food? More, what was it that they rejoiced over, that long dark thing which lay so quiet upon the ground? It did not look like a head of game, and it could scarcely be a crocodile, yet clearly it was food of some sort, for they were sharpening the stone knives in order to cut it up.

While she wondered thus, one of the dreadful-looking little creatures advanced to the fire, and taking from it a burning bough, held it over the thing that lay upon the ground, to give light to a companion who was about to do something to it with the stone knife. Next instant Nanea drew back her head from the hole, a stifled shriek upon her lips. She saw what it was now—it was the body of a man. Yes, and these were no ghosts; they were cannibals of whom when she was little, her mother had told her tales to keep her from wandering away from home.

But who was the man they were about to eat? It could not be one of themselves, for his stature was much greater. Oh! now she knew; it must be Nahoon, who had been killed up yonder, and whose dead body the waters had brought down to the haunted forest as they had brought her alive. Yes, it must be Nahoon, and she would be forced to see her husband devoured before her eyes. The thought of it overwhelmed her. That he should die by order of the king was natural, but that he should be buried thus! Yet what could she do to prevent it? Well, if it cost her her life, it should be prevented. At the worst they could only kill and eat her also, and now that Nahoon and her father were gone, being untroubled by any religious or spiritual hopes and fears, she was not greatly concerned to keep her own breath in her.

Slipping through the hole in the tree, Nanea walked quietly towards the cannibals—not knowing in the least what she should do when she reached them. As she arrived in line with the fire this lack of programme came home to her mind forcibly, and she paused to reflect. Just then one of the cannibals looked up to see a tall and stately figure wrapped in a white garment which, as the flame-light flickered on it, seemed now to advance from the dense background of shadow, and now to recede into it. The poor savage wretch was holding a stone knife in his teeth when he beheld her, but it did not remain there long, for opening his great jaws he uttered the most terrified and piercing yell that Nanea had ever heard. Then the others saw her also, and presently the forest was ringing with shrieks of fear. For a few seconds the outcasts stood and gazed, then they were gone this way and that, bursting their path through the undergrowth like startled jackals. The Esemkofu of Zulu tradition had been routed in their own haunted home by what they took to be a spirit.

Poor Esemkofu! they were but miserable and starving bushmen who, driven into that place of ill omen many years ago, had adopted this means, the only one open to them, to keep the life in their wretched bodies. Here at least they were unmolested, and as there was little other food to be found amid that wilderness of trees, they took what the river brought them. When executions were few in the Pool of Doom, times were hard for them indeed—for then they were driven to eat each other. That is why there were no children.

As their inarticulate outcry died away in the distance, Nanea ran forward to look at the body that lay on the ground, and staggered back with a sigh of relief. It was not Nahoon, but she recognised the face for that of one of the party of executioners. How did he come here? Had Nahoon killed him? Had Nahoon escaped? She could not tell, and at the best it was improbable, but still the sight of this dead soldier lit her heart with a faint ray of hope, for how did he come to be dead if Nahoon had no hand in his death? She could not bear to leave him lying so near her hiding-place, however; therefore, with no small toil, she rolled the corpse back into the water, which carried it swiftly away. Then she returned to the tree, having first replenished the fire, and awaited the light.

At last it came—so much of it as ever penetrated this darksome den—and Nanea, becoming aware that she was hungry, descended from the tree to search for food. All day long she searched, finding nothing, till towards sunset she remembered that on the outskirts of the forest there was a flat rock where it was the custom of those who had been in any way afflicted, or who considered themselves or their belongings to be bewitched, to place propitiatory offerings of food wherewith the Esemkofu and Amalhosi were supposed to satisfy their spiritual cravings. Urged by the pinch of starvation, to this spot Nanea journeyed rapidly, and found to her joy that some neighbouring kraal had evidently been in recent trouble, for the Rock of Offering was laden with cobs of corn, gourds of milk, porridge and even meat. Helping herself to as much as she could carry, she returned to her lair, where she drank of the milk and cooked meat and mealies at the fire. Then she crept back into the tree, and slept.

For nearly two months Nanea lived thus in the forest, since she could not venture out of it—fearing lest she should be seized, and for a second time taste of the judgment of the king. In the forest at least she was safe, for none dared enter there, nor did the Esemkofu give her further trouble. Once or twice she saw them, but on each occasion they fled from her presence—seeking some distant retreat, where they hid themselves or perished. Nor did food fail her, for finding that it was taken, the pious givers brought it in plenty to the Rock of Offering.

But, oh! the life was dreadful, and the gloom and loneliness coupled with her sorrows at times drove her almost to insanity. Still she lived on, though often she desired to die, for if her father was dead, the corpse she had found was not the corpse of Nahoon, and in her heart there still shone that spark of home. Yet what she hoped for she could not tell.

When Philip Hadden reached civilised regions, he found that war was about to be declared between the Queen and Cetywayo, King of the Amazulu; also that in the prevailing excitement his little adventure with the Utrecht store-keeper had been overlooked or forgotten. He was the owner of two good buck-waggons with spans of salted oxen, and at that time vehicles were much in request to carry military stores for the columns which were to advance into Zululand; indeed the transport authorities were glad to pay £90 a month for the hire of each waggon and to guarantee the owners against all loss of cattle. Although he was not desirous of returning to Zululand, this bait proved too much for Hadden, who accordingly leased out his waggons to the Commissariat, together with his own services as conductor and interpreter.

He was attached to No. 3 column of the invading force, which it may be remembered was under the immediate command of Lord Chelmsford, and on the 20th of January, 1879, he marched with it by the road that runs from Rorke's Drift to the Indeni forest, and encamped that night beneath the shadow of the steep and desolate mountain known as Isandhlwana.

That day also a great army of King Cetywayo's, numbering twenty thousand men and more, moved down from the Upindo Hill and camped upon the stony plain that lies a mile and a half to the east of Isandhlwana. No fires were lit, and it lay there in utter silence, for the warriors were "sleeping on their spears."

With that impi was the Umcityu regiment, three thousand five hundred strong. At the first break of dawn the Induna in command of the Umcityu looked up from beneath the shelter of the black shield with which he had covered his body, and through the thick mist he saw a great man standing before him, clothed only in a moocha, a gaunt wild- eyed man who held a rough club in his hand. When he was spoken to, the man made no answer; he only leaned upon his club looking from left to right along the dense array of innumerable shields.

"Who is this Silwana (wild creature)?" asked the Induna of his captains wondering.

The captains stared at the wanderer, and one of them replied, "This is Nahoon-ka-Zomba, it is the son of Zomba who not long ago held rank in this regiment of the Umcityu. His betrothed, Nanea, daughter of Umgona, was killed together with her father by order of the Black One, and Nahoon went mad with grief at the sight of it, for the fire of Heaven entered his brain, and mad he has wandered ever since."

"What would you here, Nahoon-ka-Zomba?" asked the Induna.

Then Nahoon spoke slowly. "My regiment goes down to war against the white men; give me a shield and a spear, O Captain of the king, that I may fight with my regiment, for I seek a face in the battle."

So they gave him a shield and a spear, for they dared not turn away one whose brain was alight with the fire of Heaven.

When the sun was high that day, bullets began to fall among the ranks of the Umcityu. Then the black-shielded, black-plumed Umcityu arose, company by company, and after them arose the whole vast Zulu army, breast and horns together, and swept down in silence upon the doomed British camp, a moving sheen of spears. The bullets pattered on the shields, the shells tore long lines through their array, but they never halted or wavered. Forward on either side shot out the horns of armed men, clasping the camp in an embrace of steel. Then as these began to close, out burst the war cry of the Zulus, and with the roar of a torrent and the rush of a storm, with a sound like the humming of a billion bees, wave after wave the deep breast of the impi rolled down upon the white men. With it went the black-shielded Umcityu and with them went Nahoon, the son of Zomba. A bullet struck him in the side, glancing from his ribs, he did not heed; a white man fell from his horse before him, he did not stab, for he sought but one face in the battle.

He sought—and at last he found. There, among the waggons where the spears were busiest, there standing by his horse and firing rapidly was Black Heart, he who had given Nanea his betrothed to death. Three soldiers stood between them, one of them Nahoon stabbed, and two he brushed aside; then he rushed straight at Hadden.

But the white man saw him come, and even through the mask of his madness he knew Nahoon again, and terror took hold of him. Throwing away his empty rifle, for his ammunition was spent, he leaped upon his horse and drove his spurs into its flanks. Away it went among the carnage, springing over the dead and bursting through the lines of shields, and after it came Nahoon, running long and low with head stretched forward and trailing spear, running as a hound runs when the buck is at view.

Hadden's first plan was to head for Rorke's Drift, but a glance to the left showed him that the masses of the Undi barred that way, so he fled straight on, leaving his path to fortune. In five minutes he was over a ridge, and there was nothing of the battle to be seen, in ten all sounds of it had died away, for few guns were fired in the dread race to Fugitive's Drift, and the assegai makes no noise. In some strange fashion, even at this moment, the contrast between the dreadful scene of blood and turmoil that he had left, and the peaceful face of Nature over which he was passing, came home to his brain vividly. Here birds sang and cattle grazed; here the sun shone undimmed by the smoke of cannon, only high up in the blue and silent air long streams of vultures could be seen winging their way to the Plain of Isandhlwana.

The ground was very rough, and Hadden's horse began to tire. He looked over his shoulder—there some two hundred yards behind came the Zulu, grim as Death, unswerving as Fate. He examined the pistol in his belt; there was but one undischarged cartridge left, all the rest had been fired and the pouch was empty. Well, one bullet should be enough for one savage: the question was should he stop and use it now? No, he might miss or fail to kill the man; he was on horseback and his foe on foot, surely he could tire him out.

A while passed, and they dashed through a little stream. It seemed familiar to Hadden. Yes, that was the pool where he used to bathe when he was the guest of Umgona, the father of Nanea; and there on the knoll to his right were the huts, or rather the remains of them, for they had been burnt with fire. What chance had brought him to this place, he wondered; then again he looked behind him at Nahoon, who seemed to read his thoughts, for he shook his spear and pointed to the ruined kraal.

On he went at speed for here the land was level, and to his joy he lost sight of his pursuer. But presently there came a mile of rocky ground, and when it was past, glancing back he saw that Nahoon was once more in his old place. His horse's strength was almost spent, but Hadden spurred it forward blindly, whither he knew not. Now he was travelling along a strip of turf and ahead of him he heard the music of a river, while to his left rose a high bank. Presently the turf bent inwards and there, not twenty yards away from him, was a Kaffir hut standing on the brink of a river. He looked at it, yes, it was the hut of that accursed inyanga, the Bee, and standing by the fence of it was none other than the Bee herself. At the sight of her the exhausted horse swerved violently, stumbled and came to the ground, where it lay panting. Hadden was thrown from the saddle but sprang to his feet unhurt.

"Ah! Black Heart, is it you? What news of the battle, Black Heart?" cried the Bee in a mocking voice.

"Help me, mother, I am pursued," he gasped.

"What of it, Black Heart, it is but by one tired man. Stand then and face him, for now Black Heart and White Heart are together again. You will not? Then away to the forest and seek shelter among the dead who await you there. Tell me, tell me, was it the face of Nanea that I saw beneath the waters a while ago? Good! bear my greetings to her when you two meet in the House of the Dead."

Hadden looked at the stream; it was in flood. He could not swim it, so followed by the evil laugh of the prophetess, he sped towards the forest. After him came Nahoon, his tongue hanging from his jaws like the tongue of a wolf.

Now he was in the shadow of the forest, but still he sped on following the course of the river, till at length his breath failed, and he halted on the further side of a little glade, beyond which a great tree grew. Nahoon was more than a spear's throw behind him; therefore he had time to draw his pistol and make ready.

"Halt, Nahoon," he cried, as once before he had cried; "I would speak with you."

The Zulu heard his voice, and obeyed.

"Listen," said Hadden. "We have run a long race and fought a long fight, you and I, and we are still alive both of us. Very soon, if you come on, one of us must be dead, and it will be you, Nahoon, for I am armed and as you know I can shoot straight. What do you say?"

Nahoon made no answer, but stood still at the edge of the glade, his wild and glowering eyes fixed on the white man's face and his breath coming in short gasps.

"Will you let me go, if I let you go?" Hadden asked once more. "I know why you hate me, but the past cannot be undone, nor can the dead be brought to earth again."

Still Nahoon made no answer, and his silence seemed more fateful and more crushing than any speech; no spoken accusation would have been so terrible in Hadden's ear. He made no answer, but lifting his assegai he stalked grimly toward his foe.

When he was within five paces Hadden covered him and fired. Nahoon sprang aside, but the bullet struck him somewhere, for his right arm dropped, and the stabbing spear that he held was jerked from it harmlessly over the white man's head. But still making no sound, the Zulu came on and gripped him by the throat with his left hand. For a space they struggled terribly, swaying to and fro, but Hadden was unhurt and fought with the fury of despair, while Nahoon had been twice wounded, and there remained to him but one sound arm wherewith to strike. Presently forced to earth by the white man's iron strength, the soldier was down, nor could he rise again.

"Now we will make an end," muttered Hadden savagely, and he turned to seek the assegai, then staggered slowly back with starting eyes and reeling gait. For there before him, still clad in her white robe, a spear in her hand, stood the spirit of Nanea!

"Think of it," he said to himself, dimly remembering the words of the inyanga, "when you stand face to face with the ghost of the dead in the Home of the Dead."

There was a cry and a flash of steel; the broad spear leapt towards him to bury itself in his breast. He swayed, he fell, and presently Black Heart clasped that great reward which the word of the Bee had promised Him.

"Nahoon! Nahoon!" murmured a soft voice, "awake, it is no ghost, but I—Nanea—I, your living wife, to whom my Ehlose[*] has given it me to save you."

[*] Guardian Spirit.

Nahoon heard and opened his eyes to look and his madness left him.

"Welcome, wife," he said faintly, "now I will live since Death has brought you back to me in the House of the Dead."

To-day Nahoon is one of the Indunas of the English Government in Zululand, and there are children about his kraal. It was from the lips of none other than Nanea his wife that the teller of this tale heard its substance.

The Bee also lives and practises as much magic as she dares under the white man's rule. On her black hand shines a golden ring shaped like a snake with ruby eyes, and of this trinket the Bee is very proud.

The Blue Curtains

Chapter I

In his regiment familiarly they called him "Bottles," nobody quite knew why. It was, however, rumoured that he had been called "Bottles" at Harrow on account of the shape of his nose. Not that his nose was particularly like a bottle, but at the end of it was round and large and thick. In reality, however, the sobriquet was more ancient than that, for it had belonged to the hero of this story from babyhood. Now, when a man has a nickname, it generally implies two things: first, that he is good-tempered, and, secondly, that he is a good fellow. Bottles, alias John George Peritt, of a regiment it is unnecessary to name, amply justified both these definitions, for a kindlier-tempered or better fellow never breathed. But unless a thick round nose, a pair of small light-coloured eyes, set under bushy brows, and a large but not badly shaped mouth can be said to constitute beauty, he was not beautiful. On the other hand, however, he was big and well-formed, and a pleasant-mannered if a rather silent companion.

Many years ago Bottles was in love; all the regiment knew it, he was so very palpably and completely in love. Over his bed in his tidy quarters hung the photograph of a young lady who was known to be the young lady; which, when the regiment, individually and collectively, happened to see it, left no doubt in its mind as to their comrade's taste. It was evident even from that badly-coloured photograph that Miss Madeline Spenser had the makings of a lovely figure and a pair of wonderful eyes. It was said, however, that she had not a sixpence; and as our hero had but very few, the married ladies of the battalion used frequently to speculate how Mr. Peritt would "manage" when it came to matrimony.

At this date the regiment was quartered in Maritzburg, Natal, but its term of foreign service had expired, and it expected to be ordered home immediately.

One morning Bottles had been out buck hunting with the scratch pack kept in those days by the garrison at Maritzburg. The run had been a good one, and after a seven or eight-mile gallop over the open country they had actually killed their buck—a beautiful Oribe. This was a thing that did not often happen, and Bottles returned filled with joy and pride with the buck fastened behind his saddle, for he was whip to the pack. The hounds had met at dawn, and it was nine o'clock or so, when, as he was riding hot and tired up the shadier side of broad and dusty Church Street, a gun fired at the Fort beyond Government House announced the arrival of the English mail.

With a beaming smile—for to him the English mail meant one if not two letters from Madeline, and possibly the glad news of sailing orders—he pushed on to his quarters, tubbed and dressed, and then went down to the mess-house for breakfast, expecting to find the letters delivered. But the mail was a heavy one, and he had ample time to eat his breakfast, also to sit and smoke a pipe upon the pleasant verandah under the shade of the bamboos and camellia bushes before the orderly arrived with the bag. Bottles went at once into the room that opened on to the veranda and stood by calmly, not being given to betraying his emotions, while slowly and clumsily the mess sergeant sorted the letters. At last he got his packet—it only consisted of some newspapers and a single letter—and went away back to his seat on the veranda, feeling rather disappointed, for he had expected to hear from his only brother as well as from his lady-love. Having relit his pipe—for he was of a slow and deliberate mind, and it rather enhances a pleasure to defer it a little—and settled himself in the big chair opposite the camellia bush just now covered with sealing-wax-like blooms, he opened his letter and read:—

"My dear George—"

"Good heavens!" he thought to himself, "what can be the matter? She always calls me 'Darling Bottles!'"

"My dear George," he began again, "I hardly know how to begin this letter—I can scarcely see the paper for crying, and when I think of you reading it out in that horrid country it makes me cry more than ever. There! I may as well get it out at once, for it does not improve by keeping—it is all over between you and me, my dear, dear old Bottles."

"All over!" he gasped to himself.

"I hardly know how to tell the miserable story," went on the letter, "but as it must be told I suppose I had better begin from the beginning. A month ago I went with my father and my aunt to the Hunt Ball at Atherton, and there I met Sir Alfred Croston, a middle-aged gentleman, who danced with me several times. I did not care about him much, but he made himself very agreeable, and when I got home aunt—you know her nasty way—congratulated me on my conquest. Well, next day he came to call, and papa asked him to stop to dinner, and he took me in, and before he went away he told me that he was coming to stop at the George Inn to fish for trout in the lake. After that he came here every day, and whenever I went out walking he always met me, and really was kind and nice. At last one day he asked me to marry him, and I was very angry and told him that I was engaged to a gentleman in the army, who was in South Africa. He laughed, and said South Africa was a long way off, and I hated him for it. That evening papa and aunt set on me—you know they neither of them liked our engagement—and told me that our affair was perfectly silly, and that I must be mad to refuse such an offer. And so it went on, for he would not take 'no' for an answer; and at last, dear, I had to give in, for they gave me no peace, and papa implored me to consent for his sake. He said the marriage would be the making of him, and now I suppose I am engaged. Dear, dear George, don't be angry with me, for it is not my fault, and I suppose after all we could not have got married, for we have so little money. I do love you, but I can't help myself. I hope you won't forget me, or marry anybody else—at least, not just at present—for I cannot bear to think about it. Write to me and tell me you won't forget me, and that you are not angry with me. Do you want your letters back? If you burn mine that will do. Good-bye, dear! If you only knew what I suffer! It is all very well to talk like aunt does about settlements and diamonds, but they can't make up to me for you. Good-bye, dear, I cannot write any more because my head aches so.—Ever yours,

"Madeline Spenser."

When George Peritt, alias Bottles, had finished reading and re-reading this letter, he folded it up neatly and put it, after his methodical fashion, into his pocket. Then he sat and stared at the red camellia blooms before him, that somehow looked as indistinct and misty as though they were fifty yards off instead of so many inches.

"It is a great blow," he said to himself. "Poor Madeline! How she must suffer!"

Presently he rose and walked—rather unsteadily, for he felt much upset—to his quarters, and, taking a sheet of notepaper, wrote the following letter to catch the outgoing mail:—

"My dear Madeline,—I have got your letter putting an end to our engagement. I don't want to dwell on myself when you must have so much to suffer, but I must say that it has been, and is, a great blow to me. I have loved you for so many years, ever since we were babies, I think; it does seem hard to lose you now after all. I thought that when we got home I might get the adjutancy of a militia regiment, and that we might have been married. I think we might have managed on five hundred a year, though perhaps I have no right to expect you to give up comforts and luxuries to which you are accustomed; but I am afraid that when one is in love one is apt to be selfish. However, all that is done with now, as, of course, putting everything else aside, I could not think of standing in your way in life. I love you much too well for that, dear Madeline, and you are too beautiful and delicate to be the wife of a poor subaltern with little beside his pay. I can honestly say that I hope you will be happy. I don't ask you to think of me too often, as that might make you less so, but perhaps sometimes when you are quiet you will spare your old lover a thought or two, because I am sure nobody could care for you more than I do. You need not be afraid that I shall forget you or marry anybody else. I shall do neither the one nor the other. I must close this now to catch the mail; I don't know that there is anything more to say. It is a hard trial—very;

but it is no good being weak and giving way, and it consoles me to think that you are 'bettering yourself' as the servants say. Good-bye, dear Madeline. May God bless you, is now and ever my earnest prayer.

"J. G. Peritt."

Scarcely was this letter finished and hastily dispatched when a loud voice was heard calling, "Bottles, Bottles, my boy, come rejoice with me; the orders have come—we sail in a fortnight;" followed by the owner of the voice, another subaltern, and our hero's bosom friend. "Why, you don't seem very elated," said he of the voice, noting his friend's dejected and somewhat dazed appearance.

"No—that is, not particularly. So you sail in a fortnight, do you?"

"'You sail?' What do you mean? Why, we all sail, of course, from the colonel down to the drummer-boy."

"I don't think that I—I am going to sail, Jack," was the hesitating answer.

"Look here, old fellow, are you off your head, or have you been liquoring up, or what?"

"No—that is, I don't think so; certainly not the first—the second, I mean."

"Then what do you mean?"

"I mean that, in short, I am sending in my papers. I like this climate —I, in short, am going to take to farming."

"Sending in your papers! Going to take to farming! And in this God-forsaken hole, too. You must be screwed."

"No, indeed. It is only ten o'clock."

"And how about getting married, and the girl you are engaged to, and whom you are looking forward so much to seeing. Is she going to take to farming?"

Bottles winced visibly.

"No, you see—in short, we have put an end to that. I am not engaged now."

"Oh, indeed," said the friend, and awkwardly departed.

Chapter II

Twelve years have passed since Bottles sent in his papers, and in twelve years many things happen. Amongst them recently it had happened that our hero's only and elder brother had, owing to an unexpected development of consumption among the expectant heirs, tumbled into a baronetcy and eight thousand a year, and Bottles himself into a modest but to him most ample fortune of as many hundred. When the news reached him he was the captain of a volunteer corps engaged in one of the numerous Basuto wars in the Cape Colony. He served the campaign out, and then, in obedience to his brother's entreaties and a natural craving to see his native land, after an absence of nearly fourteen years, resigned his commission and returned to England.

Thus it came to pass that the next scene of this little history opens, not upon the South African veld, or in a whitewashed house in some half-grown, hobbledehoy colonial town, but in a set of the most comfortable chambers in the Albany, the local and appropriate habitation of the bachelor brother aforesaid, Sir Eustace Peritt.

In a very comfortable arm-chair in front of a warm fire (for the month is November) sits the Bottles of old days—bigger, uglier, shyer than ever, and in addition, disfigured by an assegai wound through the cheek. Opposite to him, and peering at him occasionally with fond curiosity through an eyeglass, is his brother, a very different stamp of man. Sir Eustace Peritt is a well-preserved, London-looking gentleman, of apparently any age between thirty and fifty. His eye is so bright, his figure so well preserved, that to judge from appearances alone you would put him down to the former age. But when you come to know him so as to be able to measure his consummate knowledge of the world, and to have the opportunity of reflecting upon the good-natured but profound cynicism which pleasantly pervades his talk as absolutely as the flavour of lemon pervades rum punch, you would be inclined to assign his natal day to a much earlier date. In reality he was forty, neither more nor less, and had both preserved his youthful appearance and gained the mellowness of his experience by a judicious use of the opportunities of life.

"Well, my dear George," said Sir Eustace, addressing his brother—determined to take this occasion of meeting after so long a time to be rid of the nickname "Bottles," which he hated—"I haven't had such a pleasure for years."

"As—as what?"

"As meeting you again, of course. When I saw you on the vessel I knew you at once. You have not changed at all, unless expansion can be called a change."

"Nor have you, Eustace, unless contraction can be called a change. Your waist used to be bigger, you know."

"Ah, George, I drank beer in those days; it is one of things of which I have lived to see the folly. In fact, there are not many things of which I have not lived to see the folly."

"Except living itself, I suppose?"

"Exactly—except living. I have no wish to follow the example of our poor cousins," he answered with a sigh, "to whose considerate behaviour, however," he added, brightening, "we owe our present improved position." Then came a pause.

"Fourteen years is a long time, George; you must have had a rough time of it."

"Yes, pretty rough. I have seen a good deal of irregular service, you know."

"And never got anything out of it, I suppose?"

"Oh, yes; I have got my bread and butter, which is all I am worth."

Sir Eustace looked at his brother doubtfully through his eyeglass. "You are modest," he said; "that does not do. You must have a better opinion of yourself if you want to get on in the world."

"I don't want to get on. I am quite content to earn a living, and I am modest because I have seen so many better men fare worse."

"But now you need not earn a living any more. What do you propose to do? Live in town? I can set you going in a very good lot. You will be quite a lion with that hole in your cheek—by the way, you must tell me the story. And then, you see, if anything happens to me you stand in for the title and estates. That will be quite enough to float you."

Bottles writhed uneasily in his chair. "Thank you, Eustace; but really I must ask you—in short, I don't want to be floated or anything of the sort. I would rather go back to South Africa and my volunteer corps. I would indeed. I hate strangers, and society, and all that sort of thing. I'm not fit for it like you."

"Then what do you mean to do—get married and live in the country?"

Bottles coloured a little through his sun-tanned skin—a fact that did not escape the eyeglass of his observant brother. "No, I am not going to get married, certainly not."

"By the way," said Sir Eustace carelessly, "I saw your old flame, Lady Croston, yesterday, and told her you were coming home. She makes a charming widow."

"What!" ejaculated his brother, slowly raising himself out of his chair in astonishment. "Is her husband dead?"

"Dead? Yes, died a year ago, and a good riddance too. He appointed me one of his executors; I am sure I don't know why, for we never liked each other. I think he was the most disagreeable fellow I ever knew. They say he gave his wife a roughish time of it occasionally. Serve her right, too."

"Why did it serve her right?"

Sir Eustace shrugged his shoulders.

"When a heartless girl jilts the fellow she is engaged to in order to sell herself to an elderly beast, I think she deserves all she gets. This one did not get half enough; indeed, she has made a good thing of it—better than she expected."

His brother sat down again before he answered in a constrained voice, "Don't you think you are rather hard on her, Eustace?"

"Hard on her? No, not a bit of it. Of all the worthless women that I know, I think Madeline Croston is the most worthless. Look how she treated you."

"Eustace," broke in his brother almost sharply, "if you don't mind, I wish you would not talk of her like that to me. I can't—in short, I don't like it."

Sir Eustace's eyeglass dropped out of Sir Eustace's eye—he had opened it so wide to stare at his brother. "Why, my dear fellow," he ejaculated, "you don't mean to tell me you still care for that woman?"

His brother twisted his great form about uncomfortably in the low chair as he answered, "I don't know, I'm sure, about caring for her, but I don't like to hear you say such things about her."

Sir Eustace whistled softly. "I am sorry if I offended you, old fellow," he said. "I had no idea that it was still a sore point with you. You must be a faithful people in South Africa. Here the 'holy feelings of the heart' are shorter lived. We wear out several generations of them in twelve years."

Chapter III

Bottles did not go to bed till late that night. Long after Sir Eustace —who, always careful of his health, never stopped up late if he could avoid it—had vanished, yawning, his brother sat smoking pipe after pipe and thinking. He had sat many times in the same way on a wagon-box in the African veld, or up where the moonlight turned the falls of the Zambesi into a rushing cataract of silver, or alone in his tent when all the camp was sleeping round him. It was a habit of this queer, silent man to sit and think for hours at night, and arose to a great extent from an incapacity to sleep, that was the weak point in his constitution.

As for his meditations, they were various, but mostly the outcome of a curious speculative side to his nature, which he never revealed to the outside world. Dreams of a happiness of which heretofore his hard life had given him no glimpse; semi-mystical, religious meditations upon the great unknown around us; and grand schemes for the regeneration of mankind—all formed part of them.

But there was one central thought, the fixed star of his mind, round which all the others continually revolved, taking their light and colour from it, and that was the thought of Madeline Croston, the woman to whom he had been engaged. Years and years had passed since he had seen her face, and yet it was always present to him. Beyond the occasional mention of her name in some society paper—several of which, by the way, he took in for years and conscientiously searched on the chance of finding it—till this evening he had never even seen it or heard it spoken; and yet with all the tenacity of his strong, deep nature he clung to her dear memory. That she had left him to marry another man weighed as nothing in the balance of his love. Once she had loved him, and thereby he was repaid for the devotion of his life. He had no ambitions. Madeline had been his great ambition; and when that had fallen, all the others had fallen with it, even to the dust. He simply did his duty, whatever it might be, as well as in him lay, without fear of blame or hope of praise—shunning men, and never, if he could avoid it, speaking to a woman, content to earn his livelihood, and for the rest rendered colourless by his secret and pathetic passion.

And now it appeared that Madeline was a widow, which meant—and his heart beat fast at the thought—that she was a free woman. Madeline was a free woman, and he was within a few minutes' walk of her. No thousands of miles of ocean rolled between them now. He rose, went to the table, and consulted a Red book that lay on it. There was the address—a house in Grosvenor Street. Overcome by an uncontrollable impulse, he went out of the room. Going to his own he found his mackintosh and a round hat, and softly left the house. It was then past two in the morning, pouring with rain, and blowing hard.

He had been a little in London as a lad and remembered the main thoroughfares, so had no great difficulty in finding his way up Piccadilly till he came to Park Lane, into which the Red book told him Grosvenor Square opened. But to find Grosvenor Street itself was a more difficult matter, and at such a time on such a night there was naturally nobody to ask—least of all a policeman. At last he found it, and hurried on down the street with a quickening pulse. What he was hurrying to he could not tell, but that over-mastering impulse forced him on quicker and quicker yet.

Suddenly he halted, and examined the number of one of the houses by the faint and struggling light from the nearest lamp. It was her house; now there was nothing between them but a few feet of space and fourteen inches of brickwork. He crossed over to the other side of the street, and looked up at the house, but could scarcely make it out through the driving rain. There was no light in the house, and no sign of life about the street. But there were both light and life in the heart of this watcher. All the pulses of his blood were astir, keeping time with the commotion of his mind. He stood there in the shadow, gazing at the murky house, heedless of the bitter wind and pelting rain, and felt his life and spirit pass out of his control into an unknown dominion. The storm that raged around him was nothing to the convulsion of his inner self in that hour of madness, which was yet happiness. Yet as it had arisen thus suddenly, so with equal swiftness it died away, and left him standing there with a chill sense of folly in his mind and of the bitter weather in his body; for on such a night a mackintosh and a dress coat were not adapted to keep the most ardent lover warm. He shivered, and turning, made his way back to Albany, feeling heartily ashamed of himself and his midnight expedition, and heartily glad that no one knew of it except himself.

On the following day Bottles—for convenience' sake we still call him by his old nickname—was obliged to see a lawyer with reference to the money which he had inherited, and to search for a box which had gone astray aboard the steamer; also to buy a tall hat, such as he had not worn for fourteen years; so that between one thing and another it was half-past four before he got back to the Albany. Here he donned the new hat, which did not fit very well, and a new black coat which fitted so well that it seemed to cut into his large frame in every possible direction, and departed, furiously struggling with a pair of gloves, also new, for Grosvenor Street.

A quarter of an hour's walk, for he knew the road this time, brought him to the house. Glancing for a while at the spot where he had stood on the previous night, he walked up the steps and pulled the bell. Though he looked bold enough outwardly—indeed, rather imposing than otherwise—with his broad shoulders and the great scar on his bronzed face, his breast was full of terrors. In these, however, he had not much time to indulge, for a footman, still decked in the trappings of vicarious grief, opened the door with the most startling promptitude, and he was ushered upstairs into a small but richly furnished room.

Madeline was not in the room, though to judge from the lace handkerchief lying on the floor by a low chair, and the open novel on a little wicker table alongside, she had not left it long. The footman departed, saying, in a magnificent undertone, that "her ladyship" should be informed, and left our hero to enjoy his sensations. Being one of those people whom suspense of any sort makes fidgety, he employed himself in looking at the pictures and china, even going so far as to walk to a pair of very heavy blue velvet curtains that apparently communicated with another room, and peep through them at a much larger apartment of which the furniture was done up in ghostly-looking bags.

Retreating from this melancholy sight, finally he took up a position on the hearthrug and waited. Would she be angry with him for coming? he wondered. Would it recall things she had rather forget? But perhaps she had already forgotten them—it was so long ago. Would she be very much changed? Perhaps he should not know her. Perhaps—but here he happened to lift his eyes, and there, standing between the two blue velvet curtains, was Madeline, now a woman in the full splendour of a remarkable beauty, and showing as yet, at any rate in that dull November twilight, no traces of her years. There she stood, her large dark eyes fixed upon him with a look of wistful curiosity, her shapely lips just parted to speak, and her bosom gently heaving, as though with trouble.

Poor Bottles! One look was enough. There was no chance of his attaining the blessed haven of disillusionment. In five seconds he was farther out to sea than ever. When she knew that he had seen her she dropped her eyes a little—he saw the long curved lashes appear against her cheek, and moved forward.

"How do you do?" she said softly, extending her slim, cool hand.

He took the hand and shook it, but for the life of him could think of nothing to say. Not one of the little speeches he had prepared would come into his mind. Yet the desperate necessity of saying something forced itself upon him.

"How do you do?" he ejaculated with a jerk. "It—it's very cold, isn't it?"

This remark was such an utter and ludicrous fiasco that Lady Croston could not choose but laugh a little.

"I see," she said, "that you have not got over your shyness."

"It is a long while since we met," he blurted out.

"I am very glad to see you," was her simple answer. "Now sit down and talk to me; tell me all about yourself. Stop; before you begin—how very curious it is! Do you know I dreamed about you last night—such a curious, painful dream. I dreamed that I was asleep in my room—which indeed I was—and that it was blowing a gale and raining in torrents—which I believe it was also—so there is nothing very wonderful about that. But now comes the odd part. I dreamed that you were standing out in the rain and wind and yet looking at me as though you saw me. I could not see your face because you were in the dark, but I knew it was you. Then I woke up with a start. It was a most vivid dream. And now to-day you have come to see me after all these years."

He shifted his legs uneasily. Considering the facts of the case, her dream frightened him, which was not strange. Fortunately, at that moment the impressive footman arrived with the tea-things and asked whether he should light the lamps.

"No," said Lady Croston; "put some wood on the fire." She knew that she looked her very best in those half-lights.

Then, when she had given him his tea, delighting him by remembering that he did not like sugar, she fell to drawing him out about the wild life he had been leading.

"By the way," she said presently, "perhaps you can tell me—a few days ago I bought a book for my boy"—she had two children—"all about brave deeds and that sort of thing, and in it there was a story of a volunteer officer in South Africa (the name was not mentioned) which interested me very much. Did you ever hear of it? It was this: The officer was in command of a fort containing a force that was operating against a native chief. While he was away the chief sent a flag of truce down to the fort, which was fired on by some of the volunteers in the fort, because there was a man among the truce party against whom they had a spite. Just afterwards the officer returned, and was very angry that such a thing had been done by Englishmen, whose duty it was, he said, to teach all the world what honour meant.

"Now comes the brave part of the story. Without saying any more, and notwithstanding the entreaties of his men, who knew that in all probability he was going to a death by torture, for he was so brave that the natives had set a great price upon him, wishing to kill him and use his body for medicine, which they thought would make them as brave as he was, that officer rode out far away into the mountains with only an interpreter and a white handkerchief, till he came to the chief's stronghold. But when the natives saw him coming, holding up his white handkerchief, they did not fire at him as his men had fired at them, because they were so astonished at his bravery that they thought he must be mad or inspired. So he came straight on to the walls of the stronghold, called to the chief and begged his pardon for what had happened, and then rode away again unharmed. Shortly afterwards, the chief, having captured some of the officer's volunteers, whom in the ordinary course of affairs he would have tortured to death, sent them back again untouched, with a message to the effect that he would show the English officer that he was not the only man who could behave 'like a gentleman.' I should like to know that man. Do you know who he was?"

Bottles looked uncomfortable, as well he might, for it was an incident in his own career; but her praise and enthusiasm sent a flush of pride into his face.

"I believe it was some fellow in the Basuto War," he said, prevaricating with peculiar awkwardness.

"Oh, then it is a true story?"

"Yes—that is, it is partially true. There was nothing heroic about it. It was a necessary act if our honour as fair opponents was to continue to be worth anything."

"But who was the man?" she asked, fixing her dark eyes on him suspiciously.

"The man!" he stammered. "Oh, the man—well, in short—" and he stopped.

"In short, George," she put in, for the first time calling him by his Christian name, "that man was you, and I am so proud of you, George."

It was very hateful to him in a way, for he loathed that kind of personal adulation, even from her. He was so intensely modest he had never even reported the incident in question; it had come out in some roundabout way. Yet he could not but feel happy that she had found him out. It was a great deal to him to have moved her, and her sparkling eyes and heaving bosom showed that she was somewhat moved.

He looked up and his eyes caught hers; the room was nearly dark now, but the bright flame from the wood the servant had put on the fire played upon her face. His eyes caught hers, and there was a look in them from which he could not escape, even if he had wished to do so. She had thrown her head back so that the coronet of her glossy hair rested upon the back of her low seat, and thus, without strain, could look straight up into his face. He had risen, and was standing by the mantelpiece. A slow, sweet smile grew upon the perfect face, and the dark eyes became soft and luminous as though they shone through tears.

In another second it had ended, as she thought that it would end and had intended that it should end. The great strong man was down—yes, down on his knees before her, one trembling hand catching at the arm of her chair, and the other clasping her tapering fingers. There was no hesitation or awkwardness about him now, the greatness of his long-pent passion inspired him, and he told her all without let or stop—all that he had suffered for her sake throughout those lonely years, all his wretched hopelessness, keeping nothing back.

Much she did not understand; such a passion as this was too deep to be fathomed by her shallow lines, too soaring for her to net in her world-straitened imagination. Once or twice even his exalted notions made her smile: it seemed ridiculous, knowing the world as she did, that any man should think thus of any woman. Nor, when at length he had finished, did she attempt an answer, feeling that her strength lay in silence, for she had a poor case. At least, the only argument that she used was a purely feminine one, but perfectly effective. She bent her beautiful face towards him, and he kissed it again and again.

Chapter IV

The revulsion of feeling experienced by Bottles as he hurried back to the Albany to dress for dinner—for he was to dine with his brother at one of his clubs that night—was so extraordinary and overwhelming that it took him, figuratively speaking, off his legs. As yet his mind, so long accustomed to perpetual misfortune in this, the ruling passion of his life, could not quite grasp his luck. That he should, after all, have won back his lost Madeline seemed altogether too good to be true.

As it happened, Sir Eustace had asked one or two men to meet him, amongst them an Under-Secretary for the Colonies, who, having to prepare for a severe cross-examination in the House upon South African affairs, had jumped at the opportunity of sucking the brains of a man thoroughly acquainted with the subject. But the expectant Under-Secretary was destined to meet with a grievous disappointment, for out of Bottles came no good thing. For the most part of the dinner he sat silent, only speaking when directly addressed, and then answering so much at random that the Under-Secretary quickly came to the conclusion that Sir Eustace's brother was either a fool or that he had drunk too much.

Sir Eustace himself saw that his brother's taciturnity had spoilt his little dinner, and his temper was not improved thereby. He was not accustomed to have his dinners spoiled, and felt that, so far as the Under-Secretary was concerned, he had put himself into a false position.

"My dear George," he said in a tone of bland exasperation when they had got back to the Albany, "I wonder what can be the matter with you? I told Atherleigh that you would be able to post him up thoroughly about all this Bechuana mess, and he could not get a word out of you."

His brother absently filled his pipe before he answered:

"The Bechuanas? Oh, yes, I know all about them. I lived among them for a year."

"Then why on earth didn't you tell him what you knew? You put me in rather a false position."

"I am very sorry, Eustace," he answered humbly. "I will go and see him if you like, and explain the thing to him to-morrow. The fact of the matter is, I was thinking of something else."

Sir Eustace interrogated him with a look.

"I was thinking," he went on slowly, "about Mad—about Lady Croston."

"Oh!"

"I went to see her this afternoon, and I think, I hope, that I am going to marry her."

If Bottles expected that this great news would be received by his elder brother as such news ought to be received—with congratulatory rejoicing—he was destined to be disappointed.

"Good heavens!" ejaculated Sir Eustace shortly, letting his eyeglass drop.

"Why do you say that, Eustace?" Bottles asked uneasily.

"Because—because," answered his brother in the emphatic tone which was his equivalent for strong language, "you must be mad to think of such a thing."

"Why must I be mad?"

"Because you, still a young man, with all your life before you, deliberately propose to tie yourself up to a middle-aged and passee woman—she is extremely passee by daylight, let me tell you—who has already treated you like a dog, and is burdened with a couple of children, and who, if she marries again, will bring you very little except her luxurious tastes. But I expected this. I thought she would try to catch you with those languishing black eyes of hers. You are not the first; I know her of old."

"If," said his brother, rising in dudgeon, "you are going to abuse Madeline to me, I think I had better say good night, for we shall quarrel—which I would not do for anything."

Sir Eustace shrugged his shoulders. "Those whom the gods wish to destroy they first make mad," he muttered, as he lit his hand candle. "This is what comes of a course of South Africa."

But Sir Eustace was an amenable man. His favourite motto was "Live and let live"; and having given the matter his best consideration during the lengthy process of shaving himself on the following morning, he came to the conclusion, reluctantly enough it must be owned, that it was evident that his brother meant to have his own way, and therefore the best thing to be done was to fall in with his views and trust to the chapter of accidents to bring the thing to naught. Sir Eustace, for all his apparent worldliness and cynicism, was a good fellow at heart, and cherished a warm affection for his awkward, taciturn brother. He also cherished a great dislike for Lady Croston, whose character he thoroughly understood. He saw a good deal of her, it is true, because he happened to be one of the executors of her husband's will; and since he had come into the baronetcy it had struck him that she had developed a considerable partiality for his society.

The idea of a marriage between his brother and his brother's old flame was in every way distasteful to him. In the first place, under her husband's will, Madeline would bring, comparatively speaking, relatively little with her should she marry again. That was one objection. Another, and still more forcible one from Sir Eustace's point of view, was that at her time of life she was not likely to present the house of Peritt with an heir. Now, Sir Eustace had not the slightest intention of marrying. Matrimony was, he considered, an excellent institution, and necessary to the carrying on of the world in a respectable manner, but it was not one with which he was anxious to identify himself. Therefore, if his brother married at all, it was his earnest desire that the union should bring children to inherit the title and estates. Prominent above both these excellent reasons, stood his intense distrust and dislike of the lady.

Needs must, however, when the devil (by whom he understood Madeline) drives. He was not going to quarrel with his only brother and presumptive heir because he chose to marry a woman who was not to his taste. So he shrugged his shoulders—having finished his shaving and his reflections together—and determined to put the best possible face on his disappointment.

"Well, George," he said to his brother at breakfast, "so you are going to marry Lady Croston?"

Bottles looked up surprised. "Yes, Eustace," he answered, "if she will marry me."

Sir Eustace glanced at him. "I thought the affair was settled," he said.

Bottles rubbed his big nose reflectively as he answered, "Well, no. I don't think that marriage was mentioned. But I suppose she means to marry me. In short, I don't see how she could mean anything else."

Sir Eustace breathed more freely, guessing what had taken place. So there was as yet no actual engagement.

"When are you going to see her again?"

"To-morrow. She is engaged all to-day."

His brother took out a pocket-book and consulted it. "Then I am more fortunate than you are," he said; "I have an appointment with Lady Croston this evening after dinner. Don't look jealous, old fellow, it is only about some executor's business. I think I told you that I am one of her husband's executors, blessings on his memory. She is a peculiar woman, your inamorata, and swears that she won't trust her lawyers, so I have to do all the dirty work myself, worse luck. You had better come too."

"Shan't I be in the way?" asked Bottles doubtfully, struggling feebly against the bribe.

"It is evident, my dear fellow, that you cannot be de trop. I shall present my papers for signature and vanish. You ought to be infinitely obliged to me for giving you such a chance. We will consider that settled. We will dine together, and go round to Grosvenor Street afterwards."

Bottles agreed. Could he have seen the little scheme that was dawning in his brother's brain, perhaps he would not have assented so readily.

When her old lover went away reluctantly to dress for dinner on the previous day, Madeline Croston sat down to have a good think, and the result was not entirely satisfactory. It had been very pleasant to see him, and his passionate declaration of enduring love thrilled her through and through, and even woke an echo in her own breast. It made her proud to think that this man, who, notwithstanding his ugliness and awkwardness, was yet, her instinct told her, worth half a dozen smart London fashionables, still loved her and had never ceased to love her. Poor Bottles! she had been very fond of him once. They had grown up together, and it really gave her some cruel hours when a sense of what she owed to herself and her family had forced her to discard him.

She remembered, as she sat there this evening, how at the time she had wondered if it was worth it—if life would not be brighter and happier if she made up her mind to fight through it by her honest lover's side. Well, she could answer that question now. It had been well worth it. She had not liked her husband, it is true; but on the whole she had enjoyed a good time and plenty of money, and the power that money brings. The wisdom of her later days had confirmed the judgment of her youth. As regards Bottles himself, she had soon got over that fancy; for years she had scarcely thought of him, till Sir Eustace told her that he was coming home, and she had that curious dream about him. Now he had come and made love to her, not in a civilised, philandering sort of a way, such as she was accustomed to, but with a passion and a fire and an utter self-abandonment which, while it thrilled her nerves with a curious sensation of mingled pleasure and pain, not unlike that she once experienced at a Spanish bull-fight when she saw a man tossed, was yet extremely awkward to deal with and rather alarming.

Now, too, the old question had come up again, and what was to be done? She had sheered him off the question that afternoon, but he would want to marry her, she felt sure of that. If she consented, what were they to live on? Her own juncture, in the event of her re-marriage, would be cut down to a thousand a year—she had four now, and was pinched on that; and as for Bottles, she knew what he had—eight hundred, for Sir Eustace had told her. He was next heir to the baronetcy, it was true, but Sir Eustace looked as though he would live for ever, and besides, he might marry after all.

For a few minutes Lady Croston contemplated the possibility of existing on eighteen hundred a year, and what Chancery would give her as guardian of her children in a poky house somewhere down at Kensington. Soon she realised that the thing was not to be done.

"Unless Sir Eustace will do something for him, it is very clear that we cannot be married," she said to herself with a sigh. "However, I need not tell him that just yet, or he will be rushing back to South Africa or something."

Chapter V

Sir Eustace and his brother carried out their programme. They dined together, and about half-past nine drove round to Grosvenor Street. Here they were shown into the drawing-room by the solemn footman, who informed Sir Eustace that her ladyship was upstairs in the nursery and had left a message for him that she would be down presently.

"All right; there is no hurry," said Sir Eustace absently, and the man went downstairs.

Bottles, being nervous, was fidgeting round the room as usual, and his brother, being very much at ease, was standing with his back to the fire, and staring about him. Presently his glance lit upon the blue velvet curtains which shut off the room they were in from the larger saloon that had not been used since Lady Croston's widowhood, and an idea which had been floating about in his brain suddenly took definite shape and form. He was a prompt man, and in another second he had acted up to that idea.

"George," he said in a quick, low voice, "listen to me, and for Heaven's sake don't interrupt for a minute. You know that I do not like the idea of your marrying Lady Croston. You know that I think her worthless—no, wait a minute, don't interrupt—I am only saying what I think. You believe in her; you believe that she is in love with you and will marry you, and have good reason to believe it, have you not?"

Bottles nodded.

"Very well. Supposing that I can show you within half an hour that she is perfectly ready to marry somebody else—myself, for instance—would you still believe in her?"

Bottles turned pale. "The thing is impossible," he said.

"That is not the question. Would you still believe in her, and would you still marry her?"

"Great heavens! no."

"Good. Then I tell you what I will do for you, and it will perhaps give you some idea of how deeply I feel in the matter; I will sacrifice myself."

"Sacrifice yourself?"

"Yes. I mean that I will this very evening propose to Madeline Croston under your nose, and I bet you five pounds she accepts me."

"Impossible," said Bottles again. "Besides, if she did you don't want to marry her."

"Marry her! No, indeed. I am not mad. I shall have to get out of the scrape as best I can—always supposing my view of the lady is correct."

"Excuse me," said Bottles with a gasp, "but I must ask you—in short, have you ever been on affectionate terms with Madeline?"

"Never, on my honour."

"And yet you think she will marry you if you ask her, even after what took place with me yesterday?"

"Yes, I do."

"Why?"

"Because, my boy," replied Sir Eustace with a cynical smile, "I have eight thousand a year and you have eight hundred—because I have a title and you have none. That you may happen to be the better fellow of the two will, I fear, not make up for those deficiencies."

Bottles with a motion of his hand waved his brother's courtly compliment away, as it were, and turned on him with a set white face.

"I do not believe you, Eustace," he said. "Do you understand what you make out this lady to be when you say that she could kiss me and tell me that she loved me—for she did both yesterday—and promise to marry you to-day?"

Sir Eustace shrugged his shoulders. "I think that the lady in question has done something like that before, George."

"That was years ago and under pressure. Now, Eustace, you have made this charge; you have upset my faith in Madeline, whom I hope to marry, and I say, prove it—prove it if you can. I will stake my life you cannot."

"Don't agitate yourself, my dear fellow; and as to betting, I would not risk more than a fiver. Now oblige me by stepping behind those velvet curtains—a la 'School for Scandal'—and listening in perfect silence to my conversation with Lady Croston. She does not know that you are here, so she will not miss you. You can escape when you have had enough of it, for there is a door through on to the landing, and as we came up I noticed that it was ajar. Or if you like you can appear from between the curtains like an infuriated husband on the stage and play whatever role occasion may demand. Really the situation has a laughable side. I should enjoy it immensely if I were behind the curtain too. Come, in you go."

Bottles hesitated. "I can't hide," he said.

"Nonsense; remember how much depends on it. All is fair in love or war. Quick; here she comes."

Bottles grew flurried and yielded, scarcely knowing what he did. In another second he was in the darkened room behind the curtains, through the crack in which he could command the lighted scene before him, and Sir Eustace was back at his place before the fire, reflecting that in his ardour to extricate his brother from what he considered a suicidal engagement he had let himself in for a very pretty undertaking. Suppose she accepted him, his brother would be furious, and he would probably have to go abroad to get out of the lady's way; and suppose she refused him, he would look a fool.

Meanwhile the sweep, sweep of Madeline's dress as she passed down the stairs was drawing nearer, and in another instant she was in the room. She was beautifully dressed in silver-grey silk, plentifully trimmed with black lace, and cut square back and front so as to show her rounded shoulders. She wore no ornaments, being one of the few women who are able to dispense with them, unless indeed a red camellia pinned in the front of her dress can be called an ornament. Bottles, shivering with shame and doubt behind his curtain, marked that red camellia, and wondered of what it reminded him.

Then in a flash it all came back, the scene of years and years ago—the verandah in far-away Natal, with himself sitting on it, an open letter in his hand and staring with all his eyes at the camellia bush covered with bloom before him. It seemed a bad omen to him—that camellia in Madeline's bosom. Next second she was speaking.

"Oh, Sir Eustace, I owe you a thousand apologies. You must have been here for quite ten minutes, for I heard the front door bang when you came. But my poor little girl Effie is ill with a sore throat which has made her feverish, and she absolutely refused to go to sleep unless she had my hand to hold."

"Lucky Effie," said Sir Eustace, with his politest bow; "I am sure I can understand her fancy."

At the moment he was holding Madeline's hand himself, and gave emphasis to his words by communicating the gentlest possible pressure to it as he let it fall. But knowing his habits, she did not take much notice. Comparative strangers when Sir Eustace shook hands with them were sometimes in doubt whether he was about to propose to them or to make a remark upon the weather. Alas! it had always been the weather.

"I come as a man of business besides, and men of business are accustomed to being kept waiting," he went on.

"You are really very good, Sir Eustace, to take so much trouble about my affairs."

"It is a pleasure, Lady Croston."

"Ah, Sir Eustace, you do not expect me to believe that," laughed the radiant creature at his side. "But if you only knew how I detest lawyers, and what you spare me by the trouble you take, I am sure you would not grudge me your time."

"Do not talk of it, Lady Croston. I would do a great deal more than that for you; in fact," here he dropped his voice a little, "there are few things that I would not do for you, Madeline."

She raised her delicate eyebrows till they looked like notes of interrogation, and blushed a little. This was quite a new style for Sir Eustace. Was he in earnest? she wondered. Impossible!

"And now for business," he continued; "not that there is much business; as I understand it, you have only to sign this document, which I have already witnessed, and the stock can be transferred."

She signed the paper which he had brought in a big envelope almost without looking at it, for she was thinking of Sir Eustace's remark, and he put it back in the envelope.

"Is that all the business, Sir Eustace?" she asked.

"Yes; quite all. Now I suppose that as I have done my duty I had better go away."

"I wish to Heaven he would!" groaned Bottles to himself behind the curtains. He did not like his brother's affectionate little ways or Madeline's tolerance of them.

"Indeed, no; you had better sit down and talk to me—that is, if you have got nothing pleasanter to do."

We can guess Sir Eustace's prompt reply and Madeline's smiling reception of the compliment, as she seated herself in a low chair—that same low chair she had occupied the day before.

"Now for it," said Sir Eustace to himself. "I wonder how George is getting on?"

"My brother tells me that he came to see you yesterday," he began.

"Yes," she answered, smiling again, but wondering in her heart how much he had told him.

"Do you find him much changed?"

"Not much."

"You used to be very fond of each other once, if I remember right?" said he.

"Yes, once."

"I often think how curious it is," went on Sir Eustace in a reflective tone, "to watch the various changes time brings about, especially where the affections are concerned. One sees children at the seaside making little mounds of sand, and they think, if they are very young children, that they will find them there to-morrow. But they reckon without their tide. To-morrow the sands will have swept as level as ever, and the little boys will have to begin again. It is like that with our youthful love affairs, is it not? The tide of time comes up and sweeps them away, fortunately for ourselves. Now in your case, for instance, it is, I think, a happy thing for both of you that your sandhouse did not last. Is it not?"

Madeline sighed softly. "Yes, I suppose so," she answered.

Bottles, behind the curtains, rapidly reviewed the past, and came to a different conclusion.

"Well, that is all done with," said Sir Eustace cheerfully.

Madeline did not contradict him; she did not see her way to doing so just at present.

Then came a pause.

"Madeline," said Sir Eustace presently, in a changed voice, "I have something to say to you."

"Indeed, Sir Eustace," she answered, lifting her eyebrows again in her note of interrogation manner, "what is it?"

"It is this, Madeline—I want to ask you to be my wife."

The blue velvet curtains suddenly gave a jump as though they were assisting at at spiritualistic seance.

Sir Eustace looked at the curtains with warning in his eye.

Madeline saw nothing.

"Really, Sir Eustace!"

"I dare say I surprise you," went on this ardent lover; "my suit may seem a sudden one, but in truth it is nothing of the sort."

"O Lord, what a lie!" groaned the distracted Bottles.

"I thought, Sir Eustace," murmured Madeline in her sweet low voice, "that you told me not very long ago that you never meant to marry."

"Nor did I, Madeline, because I thought there was no chance of my marrying you" ("which I am sure I hope there isn't," he added to himself). "But—but, Madeline, I love you." ("Heaven forgive me for that!") "Listen to me, Madeline, before you answer," and he drew his chair closer to her own. "I feel the loneliness of my position, and I want to get married. I think that we should suit each other very well. At our age, now that our youth is past" (he could not resist this dig, at which Madeline winced), "probably neither of us would wish to marry anybody much our junior. I have had many opportunities lately, Madeline, of seeing the beauty of your character, and to the beauties of your person no man could be blind. I can offer you a good position, a good fortune, and myself, such as I am. Will you take me?" and he laid his hand upon hers and gazed earnestly into her eyes.

"Really, Sir Eustace," she murmured, "this is so very unexpected and sudden."

"Yes, Madeline, I know it is. I have no right to take you by storm in this way, but I trust you will not allow my precipitancy to weight against me. Take a little time to think it over—a week say" ("by which time," he reflected, "I hope to be in Algiers.") "Only, if you can, Madeline, tell me that I may hope."

She made no immediate answer, but, letting her hands fall idly in her lap, looked straight before her, her beautiful eyes fixed upon vacancy, and her mind amply occupied in considering the pros and cons of the situation. Then Sir Eustace took heart of grace; bending down, he kissed the Madonna-like face. Still there was no response. Only very gently she pushed him from her, whispering:

"Yes, Eustace, I think I shall be able to tell you that you may hope."

Bottles waited to see no more. With set teeth and flaming eyes he crept, a broken man, through the door that led on to the landing, crept down the stairs and into the hall. On the pegs were his hat and coat; he took them and passed into the street.

"I have done a disgraceful thing," he thought, "and I have paid for it."

Softly as the door closed Sir Eustace heard it; and then he too left the room, murmuring, "I shall soon come for my answer, Madeline."

When he reached the street his brother was gone.

Chapter VI

Sir Eustace did not go straight back to the Albany, but, calling a hansom, drove down to his club.

"Well," he thought to himself, "I have played a good many curious parts in my time, but I never had to do with anything like this before. I only hope George is not much cut up. His eyes ought to be opened now. What a woman—" but we will not repeat Sir Eustace's comments upon the lady to whom he was nominally half engaged.

At the club Sir Eustace met his friend the Under-Secretary, who had just escaped from the House. Thanks to information furnished to him that morning by Bottles, who had been despatched by Sir Eustace, in a penitent mood, to the Colonial Office to see him, he had just succeeded in confusing, if not absolutely in defeating, the impertinent people who "wanted to know." Accordingly he was jubilant, and greeted Sir Eustace with enthusiasm, and they sat talking together for an hour or more.

Then Sir Eustace, being, as has been said, of early habits, made his way home.

In his sitting-room he found his brother smoking and contemplating the fire.

"Hullo, old fellow!" he said, "I wish you had come to the club with me. Atherleigh was there, and is delighted with you. What you told him this morning enabled him to smash up his enemies, and as the smashing lately has been rather the other way he is jubilant. He wants you to go to see him again to-morrow. Oh, by the way, you made your escape all right. I only hope I may be as lucky. Well, what do you think of your lady-love now?"

"I think," said Bottles slowly—"that I had rather not say what I do think."

"Well, you are not going to marry her now, I suppose?"

"No, I shall not marry her."

"That is all right; but I expect that it will take me all I know to get clear of her. However, there are some occasions in life when one is bound to sacrifice one's own convenience, and this is one of them. After all, she is really very pretty in the evening, so it might have been worse."

Bottles winced, and Sir Eustace took a cigarette.

"By the way, old fellow," he said, as he settled himself in his chair again, "I hope you are not put out with me over this. Believe me, you have no cause to be jealous; she does not care a hang about me, it is only the title and the money. If a fellow who was a lord and had a thousand a year more proposed to her to-morrow she would chuck me up and take him."

"No; I am not angry with you," said Bottles; "you meant kindly, but I am angry with myself. It was not honourable to—in short, play the spy upon a woman's weakness."

"You are very scrupulous," yawned Sir Eustace; "all means are fair to catch a snake. Dear me, I nearly exploded once or twice; it was better than [yawn] any [yawn] play," and Sir Eustace went to sleep.

Bottles sat still and stared at the fire.

Presently his brother woke up with a start. "Oh, you are there, are you, Bottles?" (it was the first time he had called him by that name since his return.) "Odd thing; but do you know that I was dreaming that we were boys again, and trout-fishing in the old Cantlebrook stream. I dreamt that I hooked a big fish, and you were so excited that you jumped right into the river after it—you did once, you remember—and the river swept you away and left me on the bank; most unpleasant dream. Well, good night, old boy. I vote we go down and have some trout-fishing together in the spring. God bless you!"

"Good night," said Bottles, gazing affectionately after his brother's departing form.

Then he too rose and went to his bedroom. On a table stood a battered old tin despatch-box—the companion of all his wanderings. He opened it and took from it first a little bottle of chloral.

"Ah," he said, "I shall want you if I am to sleep again." Setting the bottle down, he extracted from a dirty envelope one or two letters and a faded photograph. It was the same that used to hang over his bed in his quarters at Maritzburg. These he destroyed, tearing them into small bits with his strong brown fingers.

Then he shut the box and sat down at the table to think, opening the sluice-gates of his mind and letting the sea of misery flow in, as it were.

This, then, was the woman whom he had forgiven and loved and honoured for all these years. This was the end and this the reward of all his devotion and of all his hopes. And he smiled in bitterness of his pain and self-contempt.

What was he to do? Go back to South Africa? He had not the heart for it. Live here? He could not. His existence had been wasted. He had lost his delusion—the beautiful delusion of his life—and he felt as though it would drive him mad, as the man whose shadow left him went mad.

He rose from the chair, opened the window, and looked out. It was a clear frosty night, and the stars shone brightly. For some while he stood looking at them; then he undressed himself. Generally, for he was different to most men, he said his prayers. For years, indeed, he had not missed doing so, any more than he had missed praying Providence in them to watch over and bless his beloved Madeline. But to-night he said no prayers. He could not pray. The three angels, Faith, Hope, and Love, whose whisperings heretofore had been ever in his ears, had taken wing, and left him as he played the eavesdropper behind those blue velvet curtains.

So he swallowed his sleeping-draught and laid himself down to rest.

When Madeline Croston heard the news at a dinner-party on the following evening she was much shocked, and made up her mind to go home early. To this day she tells the story as a frightful warning against the careless use of chloral.

H. Rider Haggard – A Short Biography

Sir Henry Rider Haggard, KBE was born on June 22nd, 1856 at Bradenham in Norfolk, England.

More familiarly known as H. Rider Haggard, he was the eighth of ten children born to Sir William Meybohm Rider Haggard, a barrister (born, incidentally, in St Petersburg, Russia), and Ella Doveton, an author, poet and daughter of a merchant in the East India Trading Company.

Haggard was initially schooled at Garsington Rectory in Oxfordshire where he studied under the tutelage of Reverend H. J. Graham. His elder brothers, who seemed to find more favour with their father, graduated from various private schools whilst Haggard was sent to Ipswich Grammar School, saving his father a considerable sum in fees.

He failed his army entrance exam, and was therefore sent to a private crammer in London in preparation for the entrance exam to the British Foreign Office, which he appears never to have sat. However, it was during his two years in London that Haggard came into contact with a circle of people interested in the study of psychical phenomena and for which he too now developed a life-long interest together with a series of enduring friendships.

In 1875, Haggard's father used his family's connections to send him to Southern Africa to take up an unpaid position as assistant to the secretary to Sir Henry Bulwer, Lieutenant-Governor of the Colony of Natal. In 1876 he was transferred to the staff of Sir Theophilus Shepstone, Special Commissioner for the Transvaal. It was in this role that Haggard was present in Pretoria in April 1877 for the official announcement of the British annexation of the Boer Republic of the Transvaal. The official who had been nominated to read out the Proclamation lost his voice and Haggard was his replacement. It was a moment in history.

Haggard was to remain in the country for six years, during which time he served as Master of the High Court of the Transvaal and an adjutant of the Pretoria Horse.

It was here that he fell in love with Mary Elizabeth "Lilly" Jackson. He hoped to marry her once he obtained more certainty in his career path.

In 1878 he became Registrar of the High Court in the Transvaal and now the time seemed opportune to write to his father to tell him of his hope to marry. The reply from his father was uncompromising. He forbade it until his son had made a proper career for himself.

The following year, 1879, Lily married Frank Archer, a well-to-do banker.

Haggard returned briefly to England to marry a friend of his sister's, Marianna Louisa Margitson, a 21 year old, in 1880, and the couple travelled to Africa together. Haggard's years in Africa had proved, at least on a writing level, rich and inspirational for him, and while still in Natal he wrote two articles for The Gentleman's Magazine describing his experiences.

Moving back to England in (and accounts here differ as to whether it was 1881 or 1882) the couple settled in Ditchingham, Norfolk, Louisa's ancestral home. Later they moved to Kessingland and established connections with the church in Bungay, Suffolk. The marriage produced four children. A son named Jack (who tragically died at age 10 of measles) and three daughters, Angela, Dorothy and Lilias. (Lilias grew to become an author and her father's biographer.)

In England Law was to be the fulcrum of his career. However, although he studied, writing was growing in its appeal to him. His first book, Cetywayo and His White Neighbours, was an account and study of Britain's policies in South Africa.

From this point his career as a writer began to take substantial hold and with it a dramatic shift to fiction. Two years later he published his first fiction, Dawn followed in 1885 by arguably his most popular novel, King Solomon's Mines—detailing the life of the adventurer Allan Quatermain. This was followed the following year, 1886, by She: A History of Adventure, which introduced the female character Ayesha. Both characters, Quatermain and Ayesha, developed a series of books about their adventures.

The study of Law now fell away entirely. He appeared also to have a keen sense of his commercial appreciation. Rather than sell the copyright of his first best-seller, King Solomon's Mines, for a £100 fee he, instead, accepted a 10% royalty. This book is also generally accepted as the first of the Lost World writing genre.

Haggard obviously thought there were many further adventures to tell and it would be hard to find a publisher who would disagree given the start he had made. Sequels soon followed. Allan Quatermain continued his epic and swash-buckling adventures in Africa whilst the sequel to She entitled Ayesha played out her adventures in Tibet. Interestingly Haggard would later extend his characters adventures around the world with Eric Brighteyes, being the basis for an epic Viking romance.

The Haggard family lived at 69 Gunterstone Road in Hammersmith, London, from mid-1885 to mid-1888. It was here that he wrote his most famous works. His time in Africa had given him the experience and atmosphere as well as several observations and friendships of the people who would so influence his fictional characters. Chief among them were the larger-than-life adventurers Frederick Selous and Frederick Russell Burnham. Both were men of Empire and huge ambition as they helped uncover the great mineral wealth of Africa, as well as the ruins of ancient lost civilisations of the continent, such as Great Zimbabwe.

Three of Haggard's books, The Wizard (1896), Black Heart and White Heart; a Zulu Idyll (1896), and Elissa; the Doom of Zimbabwe (1898), are dedicated to Burnham's daughter Nada, the first white child born in Bulawayo; she had been named after Haggard's 1892 book Nada the Lily.

As is typical of the writing of the time his novels contain many of the stereotypes associated with colonialism, yet they also sympathise, to a degree, with the native populations. Africans often play heroic roles in the novels, although the protagonists are more often than not European. The time around the turn of the century was, after all, the great sprint to Empire by many European countries intent on gaining possessions of land, people and resources.

Three of Haggard's novels were written in collaboration with his friend Andrew Lang who shared his interest in the spiritual realm and paranormal phenomena and who was also a greatly admired editor.

Haggard's stories are still widely read today. Ayesha, the female protagonist of She, has been cited as a prototype by psychoanalysts such as Sigmund Freud (in The Interpretation of Dreams) and Carl Jung. Her epithet is, of course, "She Who Must Be Obeyed" and has for decades been used tongue-in-cheek to describe the presumed balance of influence between the sexes.

As a legacy it is easy to establish Haggard, and his pioneering work, as the author of the Lost World branch of writing and its influence of such other writers as Edgar Rice Burroughs, Robert E. Howard and Talbot Mundy. The Allan Quatermain character influenced many 'serials' in Hollywood during the 30s & 40s and can readily be seen as a template for Indiana Jones, the American archaeologist and explorer and huge box office film character.

Years later, when Haggard was a successful novelist, he was contacted by his former love, Lilly Archer, née Jackson. Lily had been deserted by her husband, who had embezzled funds and fled bankrupt to Africa. Haggard installed her and her sons in a house and saw to the children's education. Lilly eventually followed her husband to Africa, where he infected her with syphilis before dying of it himself. Lilly returned to England in late 1907, where Haggard again supported her until her death on April 22nd, 1909.

Haggard also wrote about agricultural and social reform, in part inspired by his experiences in Africa, but also based on what he saw in Europe. By the end of his life, he was adamantly opposed to Bolshevism, a position that he shared with his life-long friend Rudyard Kipling. The two had found friendship upon Kipling's arrival at London in 1889 largely on the strength of their shared opinions.

Haggard was extremely interested in the social affairs of the Country and eager to play a more active part in attempting reform. In 1895 he stood unsuccessfully for Parliament as a Conservative candidate for the Eastern division of Norfolk losing by 198 votes.

Also in 1895 he served on a government commission to examine Salvation Army labour colonies. This, and his heavy involvement in agriculture reform, led to him being a member of several further commissions on land use and related affairs, work that involved several trips to the Colonies and Dominions. This work, in part, helped lead to the passage of the 1909 Development Bill.

In 1911 he served on the Royal Commission examining coastal erosion.

He was an absorbed and dedicated writer of letters to The Times, nearly one hundred were published by them and the bibliography attached below reveals much in the range of subjects he wished to bring attention to.

He was made a Knight Bachelor in 1912 and a Knight Commander of the Order of the British Empire in 1919. Haggard was a member of several clubs including the Athenaeum, Savile, and Authors' clubs.

The district of Rider in British Columbia, Canada, was named in his honour.

Henry Rider Haggard died on May 14th, 1925 at the age of 68. His ashes were buried at Ditchingham Church. His papers are held at the Norfolk Record Office.

The first chapter of his book People of the Mist (1894) is credited with inspiring the 1912 motto of the Royal Air Force (formerly the Royal Flying Corps), Per ardua ad astra. "Through adversity to the stars" (or alternately "Through struggle to the stars") it is also used by other Commonwealth air forces such as the RAAF, RCAF, RNZAF, and the SAAF.

H. Rider Haggard – A Concise Bibliography

Novels

Dawn (1884) Published in three volumes
The Witch's Head (1884) Published in three volumes
King Solomon's Mines (1885) Allan Quatermain series
She: A History of Adventure (1886) Ayesha series
Allan Quatermain (1887) Allan Quatermain series
Jess (1887)
A Tale of Three Lions (1887) Allan Quatermain series
Maiwa's Revenge, or the War of the Little Hand (1888) Allan Quatermain series
Colonel Quaritch, VC (1889) Published in three volumes
Cleopatra (1889)
Beatrice (1890)
The World's Desire (1890) Co-written with Andrew Lang
Eric Brighteyes (1891)
Nada the Lily (1892)
An Heroic Effort (1893)
Montezuma's Daughter (1893)
The People of the Mist (1894)
Heart of the World (1895)
Joan Haste (1895)
The Wizard (1896)
Doctor Therne (1898)
Swallow: A Tale of the Great Trek (1899)
Lysbeth (1901)
Pearl Maiden (1903)
Stella Fregelius: A Tale of Three Destinies (1903)
The Brethren (1904)
Ayesha: The Return of She (1905) Ayesha series
The Way of the Spirit (1906)
Benita (1906)
Fair Margaret (1907)
The Ghost Kings(1908)
The Yellow God (1908)
The Lady of Blossholme (1909)
Morning Star (1910)
Queen Sheba's Ring (1910)
Red Eve (1911)
The Mahatma and the Hare (1911)
Marie (1912) Allan Quatermain series
Child of Storm (1913) Allan Quatermain series
The Wanderer's Necklace (1914)
The Holy Flower (1915) Allan Quatermain series
The Ivory Child (1916) Allan Quatermain series
Finished (1917) Allan Quatermain series]
Love Eternal (1918)
Moon of Israel (1918)

When the World Shook (1919)
The Ancient Allan (1920) Allan Quatermain series
She and Allan (1921) Allan Quatermain series / Ayesha series
The Virgin of the Sun (1922)
Wisdom's Daughter (1923) Ayesha series
Heu-Heu (1924) Allan Quatermain series]
Queen of the Dawn (1925)
The Treasure of the Lake (1926) Allan Quatermain series
Allan and the Ice-Gods (1927) Allan Quatermain series
Mary of Marion Isle (1929)
Belshazzar (1930)

Short Story Collections

Allan's Wife and Other Tales (1889)
Black Heart and White Heart: A Zulu Idyll (1900)
Smith and the Pharaohs (1920)

Publications in Periodicals and Newspapers

A Zulu War-Dance (July 1877) The Gentleman's Magazine
A Visit to the Chief (September 1877) The Gentleman's Magazine
Hydrophobia (letter) (3 November 1885) The Times
The Land Question (letter) (28 April 1886) The Times
About Fiction (February 1887) The Contemporary Review
Mr Rider Haggard and His Critics (letter) (27 April 1887) The Times
Our Position in Cyprus (July 1887) The Contemporary Review
American Copyright (letter) (11 October 1887) The Times
On Going Back (November 1887) Longman's Magazine
Delagoa Bay (letter) (17 December 1887) The Times
South African Policy (letter) (27 December 1887) The Times
Suggested Prologue to a Dramatised Version of She (March 1888) Longman's Magazine
Mr. Meeson's Will (18 June 1888) The Illustrated London News
The Wreck of the Copeland (18 August 1888) The Illustrated London News
Cleopatra (3 December 1888) The Illustrated London News
Hydrophobia and Muzzling (letter) (25 October 1889) The Times
The Annals of Natal (23 November 1889) The Saturday Review
Mummy at St Mary/Woolnoth's (letter) (25 December 1889) The Times
Mummies (letter) (27 December 1889) The Times
The Fate of Swaziland (January 1890) The New Review
In Memoriam (17 May 1890) Thompson's Seasons
American Copyright (letter) (5 June 1890) The Times
Mr Herbert Ward and Mr Stanley (10 November 1890) The Times
Nada the Lily (2 January 1892) The Illustrated London News
A New Argument Against Creation (19 December 1892) The Times
My First Book. Dawn. By H. Rider Haggard (April 1893) The Idler
The Tale of Isandlwana and Rorke's Drift (4 October 1893) The True Story Book
Lobengula (letter) (19 October 1893) The Times

The New Sentiment (letter) (6 November 1893) The Times
Wanted—Imagination (25 December 1893) The Times
The Fate of Captain Patterson's Party (28 December 1893) The Times
The Three Volume Novel (letter) (27 July 1894) The Times
The Adventures of John Gladwyn Jebb (letter) (30 October 1894) The Times
Agriculture in Norfolk (letter) (30 October 1894) The Times
The Nelson Bazaar (letter) (16 February 1895) The Times
Everything is Peaceful (letter) (20 March 1895) The Times
Lord Kimberley in Norfolk (letter) (17 April 1895) The Times
The East Norfolk Election (letter) (23 July 1895) The Times
The East Norfolk Election (letter) (29 July 1895) The Times
Wilson's Last Fight (7 October 1895) The True Story Book
The Crisis in the Transvaal (letter) (2 January 1896) The Times
The Transvaal Crisis (letter) (13 January 1896) The Times
Jameson's Surrender (letter) (14 March 1896) The Times
The Rinderpest in South Africa (letter) (5 November 1896) The Times
Mr Rider Haggard and Dr Neufeld (letter) (9 January 1899) The Times
Shrinkage of Population in Agricultural Districts (letter) (9 May 1899) The Times
The South African Crisis—An Appeal (letter) (1 July 1899) The Times
Commandant-General Joubert and Mr H Rider Haggard (letter) (8 September 1899) The Times
Anglo-African Writers' Club (17 October 1899) The Times
The War (letter) (25 October 1899) The Times
Farming in 1899 (letter) (22 December 1899) The Times
Farming in 1899 (letter) (1 January 1900) The Times
Settlement of Soldiers in South Africa (letter) (5 May 1900) The Times
1881 and 1900 (letter) (2 October 1900) The Times
Farming in 1900 (letter) (1 January 1901) The Times
Central and Associated Chambers of Agriculture (letter) (6 November 1901) The Times
Small Holdings (letter) (8 November 1901) The Times
Rural England (letter) (4 February 1903) The Times
Mr Rider Haggard on Rural Depopulation (3 May 1903) The Times
Agricultural Distress (letter) (11 June 1903) The Times
The Motor Problem (letter) (24 June 1903) The Times
Fiscal Policy and Agriculture (letter) (16 December 1903) The Times
Telepathy Between a Human Being and a Dog (letter) (21 July 1904) The Times
Telepathy Between a Human Being and a Dog (letter) (9 August 1904) The Times
Mr Rider Haggard on Small Holdings (12 September 1904) The Times
Case L.1139 Dream (October 1904) Journal of the Society for Psychical Research
Mr Rider Haggard on Agriculture (22 October 1904) The Times
Mr Rider Haggard on Rural Housing (27 October 1904) The Times
The Deserted Village (letter) (25 August 1905) The Times
Decrease of Population and the Land (letter) (6 January 1906) The Times
Prevention of Cruelty to Children (3 February 1906) The Times
The New Land and Tenure Bill (letter) (12 March 1906) The Times
Garden City Association (17 March 1906) The Times
Mr H. Rider Haggard on the Zulus (19 May 1906) The Illustrated London News
To Be Proof against British Bullets: A Zulu Incantation (19 May 1906) The Illustrated London News
Housing of the Working Classes (26 June 1906) The Times

Mr Rider Haggard on Small Holdings (4 July 1906) The Times
The Unemployed and Waste City Lands (letter) (19 July 1906) The Times
Mr Rider Haggard on the Transvaal Constitution (7 August 1906) The Times
Vanishing East Anglia (1 September 1906) The Saturday Review
The Land Grabbing at Plaistow (5 September 1906) The Times
The Land Tenure Bill (22 November 1906) The Times
Publishers and the Public (letter) (19 February 1907) The Times
The Careless Children (2 March 1907) The Saturday Review
The Government and the Land (letter) (29 April 1907) The Times
Chambers of Agriculture (2 May 1907) The Times
The Government and the Land (letter) (8 May 1907) The Times
Miss Jebb on Small Holdings (15 June 1907) Country Life
Rural Housing and Sanitation Association (27 June 1907) The Times
St Thomas Hospital Medical School (28 June 1907) The Times
The Land Question (4 July 1907) The Times
A Plea for the Sitting Tennant (letter) (12 August 1907) The Times
A Literary Coincidence (letter) (19 October 1907) The Spectator
Town Planning Conference (26 October 1907) The Times
Dr Barnardo's Homes (16 November 1907) The Times
The Proposed Agricultural Party (5 December 1907) The Times
Mr Rider Haggard and Small Holdings (10 January 1908) The Times
Mr Haggard and Children's Legislation (13 March 1908) The Times
The Drink Trade and Common Sense (letter) (2 April 1908) The Times
The Zulus: The Finest Savage Race in the World (June 1908) The Pall Mall Magazine
Sparrows (letter) (18 August 1908) The Times
Sparrows, Rats and Humanity (letter) (5 September 1908) The Times
The Letters of Queen Victoria (letter) (26 November 1908) The Times
The Romance of the World's Greatest Rivers (December 1908) Travel Magazine
Afforestation. Mr Rider Haggard's View (1 March 1909) The Times
The Late Sir Marshal Clarke (letter) (13 April 1909) The Times
Mr Rider Haggard on Agriculture (27 November 1909) The Times
Mr Rider Haggard on South Africa (11 March 1910) The Times
Why? (letter) (25 April 1910) The Times
Mr Rider Haggard on Irish Agriculture (23 May 1910) The Times
Why Not? (letter) (12 July 1910) The Times
Mr Rider Haggard on Agriculture (16 September 1910) The Times
Mr Rider Haggard on Vermin (8 November 1910) The Times
Danish High Schools (21 December 1910) The Times
Sugar Beet Growing in Norfolk (6 March 1911) The Times
Rural Denmark (letter) (22 March 1911) The Times
Rural Denmark (letter) (3 April 1911) The Times
The Copyright Bill (letter) (6 June 1911) The Times
Mr Rider Haggard on Poverty. The Burden of Civilization (15 July 1911) The Times
Mr Rider Haggard and the Public Records (28 July 1911) The Times
The Farmers' Burden (1 December 1911) The Times
Egyptian Date Farm. The Financial Aspect (11 October 1912) The Times
Umslopogaas and Makokel. Sir H. Rider Haggard on Zulu Types (letter) (16 August 1913) The Times
The Death of Mark Haggard (letter) (10 October 1914) The Times

On the Land. Old Problems and New Ways. The War—and After. (15 March 1915) The Times
Soldiers as Settlers. After-War Problem for the Empire (20 August 1915) The Times
Raids by Air. Zeppelins and Zeppelins (letter) (22 October 1915) The Times
Women's Work on the Land. A Palliative in Hard Times (letter) (29 November 1915) The Times
Women on the Land. Town Girls' Unfitness for Farm Work (letter) (9 December 1915) The Times
Soldiers as Settlers. Sir Rider Haggard's Oversea Mission (2 February 1916) The Times
Soldiers as Settlers (letter) (7 February 1916) The Times
Soldier Settlers. The Future of Rural England (letter) (10 February 1916) The Times
Farewell Luncheon to Sir Rider Haggard (March 1916) United Empire
Soldier Settlers for the Empire. Offer from Victoria (18 April 1916) The Times
Sir R Haggard's Tour. Land for Ex-Service Men (22 July 1916) The Times
Sir H. Rider Haggard's Mission. Land for Ex-Soldiers (1 August 1916) The Times
Land for Ex-Soldiers. Outline of Sir R. Haggard's Report (12 August 1916) The Times
Empire Land Settlement Deputation to the Secretary of State for the Colonies and the President of the Board of Agriculture (September 1916) United Empire
Empire Land Settlement by Sir Rider Haggard (December 1916) United Empire
A Journey through Zululand by Sir H Rider Haggard (December 1916) The Windsor Magazine
Mr Wilson's Note. British Publicity (28 December 1916) The Times
Home Produce (letter) (22 February 1917) The Times
The Milk Supply (letter) (11 April 1917) The Times
Corn Production Bill. A National Measure (letter) (13 June 1917) The Times
A Protest and a Plea. Farmers and Meat (letter) (9 October 1917) The Times
Pig-Breeding. A Subject for Municipal Enterprise (letter) (22 February 1918) The Times
The German Colonies. Interests of the Dominions (letter) (5 November 1918) The Times
Light—More Light! (letter) (19 November 1918) The Times
A Great American. Tributes to the Late Mr Roosevelt (letter) (8 January 1919) The Times
Shut the Door (letter) (10 March 1919) The Times
Population and Housing. Emigration v Birth Control (25 March 1919) The Times
The Ex-Kaiser (letter) (11 April 1919) The Times
Empire Birth-Rate. Sir Rider Haggard on Emigration (17 April 1919) The Times
Ex-Service Men Abroad. Warnings from California (letter) (10 May 1919) The Times
Edith Cavell (letter) (16 May 1919) The Times
The Ex-Kaiser. Uncertainties of Trial (letter) (8 July 1919) The Times
Race Suicide Peril. Western Civilization Threatened (11 October 1919) The Times
The British Cinema. Production of Reputable Films (letter) (5 November 1919) The Times
Horrors on the Film. Limits of Publicity (letter) (19 November 1919) The Times
The British Museum (letter) (24 January 1920) The Times
Air Exploration and Empire (letter) (7 February 1920) The Times
The Liberty League. A Campaign Against Bolshevism (letter) (3 March 1920) The Times
Bolshevist Peril. Counter-Propaganda (4 March 1920) The Times
The Empire's Vacant Lands. Settlers and the Food Supply (14 April 1920) The Times
Films and Happy Endings. The Tyranny of a Convention (letter) (21 April 1921) The Times
Land and its Burdens. Evil of Grinding Taxation (letter) (8 August 1921) The Times
Boy Emigrants (letter) (31 March 1922) The Times
Migration and Morals. Declining Birther Rate (7 April 1922) The Times
Labour Party's Programme. Confiscation and Class Hatred (letter) (28 October 1922) The Times
Efficient Denmark. Keeping the People on the Land (7 December 1922) The Times
The Egyptian Find. Tombs of Eighteenth Dynasty Queens (letter) (19 December 1922) The Times

King Tutankhamen. Reburial in Great Pyramid (letter) (13 February 1923) The Times
The Norfolk Dispute. A Truce while There is Time (letter) (3 April 1923) The Times
Rural Post and Telephone. Minister's Reply to Deputation (19 April 1923) The Times
Liberalism and Land Reform (letter) (1 May 1923) The Times
Small Holdings. Influence of Heredity (letter) (4 July 1923) The Times
Agricultural Parcel Post (26 July 1923) The Times
Country Houses for Sale. Empty East Anglian Mansions (letter) (14 June 1924) The Times
Plight of Agriculture (24 July 1924) The Times
Loans From the British Museum (letter) (30 July 1924) The Times
Zinovieff Letter. Mr MacDonald and a Political Plot (letter) (29 October 1924) The Times
Two Centuries of Publishing. Tributes to Messrs. Longmans (6 November 1924) The Times
Imagination and War (26 November 1924) The Times

Non-Fiction

Cetywayo and His White Neighbours (1882)
A Farmer's Year (1899)
The Last Boer War (1899)
A Winter Pilgrimage (1901)
Rural England (1902)
A Gardener's Year (1905)
The Poor and the Land (1905)
Regeneration (1910)
Rural Denmark (1911)
The Days of My Life (1926)

Film Adaptations

King Solomon's Mines

This novel has been adapted at least six times. The first version, King Solomon's Mines, directed by Robert Stevenson, premiered in 1937. The best known version premiered in 1950: King Solomon's Mines, directed by Compton Bennett and Andrew Marton, was followed in 1959 by a sequel, Watusi. In 1979 a low-budget version directed by Alvin Rakoff, King Solomon's Treasure, combined both King Solomon's Mines and Allan Quatermain in one story. The 1985 film King Solomon's Mines was a tongue-in-cheek parody of the story, with a 1987 sequel in the same vein, Allan Quatermain and the Lost City of Gold. Around the same time an Australian animated TV film came out, King Solomon's Mines. In 2008 a direct-to-video adaptation, Allan Quatermain and the Temple of Skulls, was released.

She

She has been adapted for the cinema at least ten times, and was one of the earliest films to be made, in 1899 as La Colonne de feu (The Pillar of Fire), by Georges Méliès. A 1911 version starred Marguerite Snow, a British-produced version appeared in 1916, and in 1917 Valeska Suratt appeared in a production for Fox which is lost. In 1925 a silent film of She, starring Betty Blythe, was produced with the active participation of Rider Haggard, who wrote the intertitles. This film combines elements from all the books in the series.

A decade later another cinematic version of the novels was released, featuring Helen Gahagan, Randolph Scott and Nigel Bruce. Unlike the book and the other films, this 1935 version was set in the Arctic, rather than Africa, and depicts the ancient civilisation of the story in an Art Deco style, with music by Max Steiner.

The 1965 film She was produced by Hammer Film Productions; it starred Ursula Andress as Ayesha and John Richardson as her reincarnated love, with Peter Cushing and Bernard Cribbins as other members of the expedition.

In 2001 another adaption was released direct-to-video with Ian Duncan as Leo Vincey, Ophélie Winter as Ayesha and Marie Bäumer as Roxane.

Dawn
The film Dawn was released in 1917, starring Hubert Carter and Annie Esmond.

Jess
This book was filmed in 1912, featuring Marguerite Snow, Florence La Badie and James Cruze, in 1914 with Constance Crawley and Arthur Maude, and in 1917 as Heart and Soul, starring Theda Bara in the title role.

Beatrice
The book was adapted into a 1921 Italian silent drama film called The Stronger Passion, directed by Herbert Brenon and starring Marie Doro and Sandro Salvini.

Swallow
The novel was adapted into a 1922 South African film.

Stella Fregelius
The book was adapted into a 1921 British film, Stella.

Moon of Israel
This novel was the basis of a script by Ladislaus Vajda, for film-director Michael Curtiz in his 1924 Austrian epic known as Die Sklavenkönigin (Queen of the Slaves).

www.ingramcontent.com/pod-product-compliance
Lightning Source LLC
LaVergne TN
LVHW010542100826
845148LV00013B/2571

* 9 7 8 1 7 8 5 4 3 8 3 2 5 *